PARENTS WANTED

ALSO BY GEORGE HARRAR

First Tiger
Radical Robots
Signs of the Apes, Songs of the Whales
(with Linda Harrar)

PARENTS WANTED

GEORGE HARRAR

ILLUSTRATIONS BY
DAN MURPHY

MILKWEED
EDITIONS

© 2001, Text by George Harrar
© 2001, Cover and interior art by Dan Murphy
All rights reserved. Except for brief quotations in critical articles or reviews, no part of this book may be reproduced in any manner without prior written permission from the publisher: Milkweed Editions, 1011 Washington Avenue South, Suite 300, Minneapolis, Minnesota 55415. (800) 520-6455 www.milkweed.org

Published 2001 by Milkweed Editions
Printed in Canada
Cover and interior design by Dale Cooney
Cover and interior art by Dan Murphy
Author photo by Glenn Rifkin
The text of this book is set in Scala.
04 05   5 4 3
First Edition

Special underwriting for this book was provided by the James R. Thorpe Foundation.

Milkweed Editions, a nonprofit publisher, gratefully acknowledges support for our inter-mediate fiction from Alliance for Reading funders: Ecolab Foundation; Jay and Rose Phillips Family Foundation; Target Stores; United Arts Partnership Funds. Other support has been provided by Elmer L. and Eleanor J. Andersen Foundation; Bush Foundation; Faegre and Benson Foundation; General Mills Foundation; Marshall Field's Project Imagine with support from the Target Foundation and Target Stores; McKnight Foundation; Minnesota State Arts Board through an appropriation by the Minnesota State Legislature and a grant from the National Endowment for the Arts; Norwest Foundation on behalf of Norwest Bank Minnesota; Lawrence and Elizabeth Ann O'Shaughnessy Charitable Income Trust in honor of Lawrence M. O'Shaughnessy; Oswald Family Foundation; Ritz Foundation on behalf of Mr. and Mrs. E. J. Phelps Jr.; John and Beverly Rollwagen Fund of the Minneapolis Foundation; St. Paul Companies, Inc.; U.S. Bancorp Foundation; and generous individuals.

Library of Congress Cataloging-in-Publication Data

Harrar, George, 1949–
    Parents wanted / George Harrar. — 1st ed.
        p. cm.
    Summary: Twelve-year-old Andrew, who has ADD, is adopted by new parents after years of other foster homes and desperately hopes that he will not mess up the situation.
        ISBN 1-57131-633-7 (pbk.) — ISBN 1-57131-632-9 (cloth)
        [1. Adoption—Fiction. 2. Attention-deficit hyperactivity disorder—Fiction.] I. Title.

PZ7.H2346 Par 2001
[Fic]—dc21

2001018001

This book is printed on acid-free paper.

To our son, Tony, who let us become his parents.

*I gratefully thank the Ludwig Vogelstein Foundation
for its early support of this book.*

*I also want to acknowledge the extraordinary
efforts on behalf of children made by
Lauren Frey and Kim Stevens at
Children's Services of Roxbury, Inc.,
Massachusetts Families for Kids Program.*

PARENTS WANTED

PROLOGUE

I ALWAYS THOUGHT I'd have my parents forever. I figured that no matter how much trouble I got into or they got into, we'd still be a family. But when I was ten years old they "surrendered their rights" to me, which is the legal way of saying they didn't want me anymore.

The last trouble happened when I took a knife to school. I know that's stupid, but it was a birthday present from Dad, and I was showing it off to my buddies. I got caught and suspended and sent home, but I didn't stay there. I hopped a bus downtown. I spent all of my money on video games as usual, and nobody would give me a dollar to take the bus back home. I must have asked fifty people. Then I saw this guy buying ice cream, and a dollar bill was sticking from his pocket. I figured it was going to fall out any second, so I decided to help it along.

He caught me by the arm and wouldn't let go. Then he handed me over to the police and the police handed me over to some social workers and they tried to hand me back to my mom but she said, "No thanks." She told them she'd "had it up to here with me" and put her hand up to her eyeballs to show what she meant. She said that she had tried and tried and tried with me, but I was just too hard to handle. My mom should be in the movies—that's how good an actress she is.

Anyway, the social workers believed her story that I was a big pain in the butt and started looking for my father. They found him in the Suffolk County jail. It's kind of embarrassing to say, but Dad's a thief. My homeroom teacher, Mr. Smiley, yelled at me when I wrote that on one of those family cards they make you fill out at school each year. Father's Occupation: Thief. What, did he want me to lie?

Personally, I don't think I'm so hard to handle. I'm only ninety-two pounds, which isn't very much for a twelve year old. I take after my dad in that. He's as skinny as a baseball bat. He says it's in our genes to be thin. We could eat pancakes for breakfast and pizza for lunch and double Whoppers for dinner, and we still wouldn't get fat. Mom used to say she put on weight just watching us eat. So it's not like I'm big enough to be a bully or anything. And when Dad was around, you know I didn't mess up because he has what Mom calls a "hair trigger," like a gun that doesn't take much squeezing to go off.

How much trouble did I get into? From what Mom told the social workers, you might think I tried to burn the school down. All I did was pull the fire alarm outside the basketball court one time. I had a good reason, too. Coach was going to make us climb the rope that day, and I hate climbing the rope. Every kid hates climbing the rope, but I was the only one who did something about it.

About the other stuff—the fights, the knife incident, skipping school—well, Mom exaggerated a lot. The truth is, I was a lot better being the kid in the family than she and Dad were being parents. They drank so much that the apartment smelled like beer. They fought so much that I had to stuff my ears with cotton and pull my pillow over my ears not to hear them. Mom doesn't like to cook, either, so there was never any food in the house except beer and pretzels for her and milk and cereal for me. Sometimes I had Fruit Loops for breakfast, Cap'n Crunch for lunch, and Frosted Flakes for dinner. I'm kind of sick of cereal.

Like I said, Mom and Dad didn't take very good care of me. I should really have surrendered *them,* but that's not how it works. Parents can walk into this place called DSS— that's the Department of Social Services—and sign some papers and get rid of a kid they don't want. But if the kid doesn't like all the drinking and shouting at home, he's stuck with the parents. That isn't fair.

My parents signed some papers, and now I officially belong to the state of Massachusetts, where I live. My social worker kept moving me in with different foster families, hoping I'd get along with one of them. I've been passed around like a puppy that nobody wants 'cause it keeps messing on the floor. At least nobody ever rapped me on the nose with a newspaper. Some kids I know got hit by their real parents *and* their foster parents, but nobody ever struck me except for my dad.

I finally ended up in this group residence called the Brighton Boys Home. Don't let the name fool you. It's not anything like a real home where you have your own room and you can use the phone whenever you want and you eat your food with regular knives and forks. At The Home, there are two or three of us stuffed in each ugly cement room. There's only one phone and it's in the hall. It's always busy, but I don't have anybody to call anyway. Everything's plastic so you can't hurt yourself. They have all of these stupid rules "for the safety of the children"—that's what the counselors always say. Like: No Sharps or Flames at Any Time. That means no knives or scissors or matches or lighters. What do they think, I'm going to jab myself to death with scissors or set my hair on fire? I'm not crazy—my parents are!

I've been here five months. I'm supposed to be learning how to behave for when a family adopts me. They say I'm doing pretty well, which just means I keep my mouth shut and say "Please" and "Thank you" all the time.

And I smile. I hate doing that because then everybody says I have cute dimples. I hate cute dimples. But if smiling is the only way I'm going to get out of here, that's what I'll do. I know this sounds weird, but I learned to smile from my cat. It happened the summer Dad swore off drinking and stealing and was trying to be a regular father. One day he decided I should have a pet and took me to the animal shelter to get a cat. In one of the cages was this big furry, mangy orange thing, and when I stuck my finger through the bars, he licked me. When I took him out and held him up, he started purring and licked my face. So of course that's the cat I picked.

I named him Orange. As soon as we got home Orange started hissing at us and scratching if we tried to rub him when he didn't want to be rubbed. At night while we were sleeping he sharpened his claws on the couch. He didn't chase the string that I dragged down the hall, and he fell asleep when I put a ball of catnip under his chin. He always wanted to be let outside, and he'd scratch at the door till somebody opened it for him.

One night he didn't come home. My friend Kenny said he saw a cat that looked exactly like Orange crossing the railroad tracks heading south. We never saw him again.

He was a pretty bad-acting cat, if you want to know the truth. So what I think is this: Orange was just faking being nice at the shelter so somebody would take him out of there. Otherwise they would have put him to sleep.

I learned a lot from that cat about smiling and acting nice even when you're really angry. I must be good at it, because my social worker says I'm ready now to look for someone to adopt me.

ONE

IT'S ADOPTION PARTY Number Five for Andy Fleck, the kid nobody wants.

Relax, my social worker tells me. Mix in with the adults. Don't go roller blading all night or hiding out at the video games. Let the people meet you.

Why bother? Who wants a twelve year old? Why would they? They'd have to be crazy.

And look at them. That guy's pants don't even cover his ankles. His wife has bushy red hair, like a clown. They look like they dropped in from Planet Weird. Who would want to be adopted by them?

Aren't there any normal parents in this place? I only need two—or better yet, just one 'cause you can get away with more stuff with a single parent watching you.

Okay, it's time to get real—if these people were normal, they'd be making their own babies and not trying to pick up somebody else's kid. I might as well go roller blading and . . .

Hold it—here comes a guy wearing Airwalks and a cool black shirt. The woman's got on a leather vest and a silver necklace. They're heading for the adoption books . . . yes, keep going . . . all right! They're sitting down and opening the one with me in it!

Oh man, now he's holding her hand like they're at a school dance or something. I hate that stuff. But look, Fleck, nobody's perfect. Remember the Airwalks. Okay, parent check—shirt tucked in, jeans pulled up, hair brushed back. Steady on your blades. Don't go falling on your butt right in front of them. Take a deep breath and speak up. Don't just stand there, SPEAK. "You looking for a boy?"

Did he say yes? Did she say anything? Smile the way the photographer told you. Now turn the pages, find your picture. . . . "There—that's me!"

"That's a very nice picture," she says.

"Well, the reason I'm in there—I mean, my picture's in there, I'm right here." God, Fleck, why don't you just tell them you're an idiot if you're going to talk like one? "What I mean is, I sort of need a family."

They're both staring at me. Do I have pizza smeared all over my face?

"What's your name?" he says.

"Andy. Andy Fleck."

"That's a nice name," she says.

"It's okay, I guess. I mean, I like 'Andy,' but 'Fleck' sounds like dandruff. I wouldn't mind having a different last name." Will they get the hint that I mean theirs? I have to be more direct. "So, what's *your* last name?"

"ScissorRotShe."

I swear that's what it sounded like. Can you imagine,

Andy ScissorRotShe? Maybe I better keep looking for parents.

She says, "It's a tough name to spell—S-I-Z-E-R-A-C-Y."

"If I were you," he says, "I'd hold onto your own last name."

"Can you do that, even when you're adopted?"

"Sure," he says, "if that's what you want."

Great, now we got the name stuff out of the way. But they still haven't said they're interested in a boy. Maybe they came here looking for a girl—girls get snapped up right away. Parents think they're easy because they don't get dirty and swear and break things. Girls are boring.

I have to make a good impression. "I can do a hand-stand. You want to see?" I drop to the floor to show them, but he taps my arm.

"It's a little crowded here," he says, "don't you think?"

Normally I'd do it anyway. I don't let adults boss me around. But this guy tapped my arm, he didn't grab it. And he asked me what I thought instead of ordering me. So I stand up. "Yeah, I guess I could hurt somebody if I knocked them in the head with my blades."

She smiles and says, "We have a big backyard. Maybe you could come over sometime and show us your handstand."

"That's a good idea," he says. "And if you like climbing trees, we have a million of them. What do you think?"

I can't believe this. I only met them two minutes ago and already they're talking about me visiting their house. That's really strange. How come some other kid hasn't sucked them up already? I can't see anything wrong with them. She's pretty sharp looking, for a mother, I mean. Her hair is long and curly, like Mom's before she got it cut. He seems just regular, like some guy in a commercial throwing a football around with his kids. They sure look a lot better than most of the foster parents I've been put with.

"Yeah, I could visit. All you have to do is talk to Al— I mean, Alison. She's my social worker."

"Okay, we'll do that."

It seems like we're done talking and I should go away, but then what if they don't go find Al? What if they forget about me? Or maybe they're just being nice and aren't really interested. That happens all the time at adoption parties. Adults think they're being nice pretending to be interested.

He stands up. "You know, maybe you should take us to meet your social worker right now. How does that sound?"

It sounds great, but I don't tell him that. I don't want them to think I'm desperate or anything. "I guess . . . if you want to."

"Lead on, Andy," he says, and then he puts his hand on my shoulder, just the way a father is supposed to.

TWO

FIRST VISITS MAKE me sick. I never know what to say. This is actually the second time I've met these people, but the adoption party doesn't really count because it was only for a few minutes a couple of weeks ago.

"Don't be nervous," Al says. Nervous? Why would I be nervous? Just because I finally found some parents who like me? They must like me, right? Otherwise they wouldn't have talked to Al at the party for so long. And we wouldn't be having lunch together unless she had already checked them out and they weren't crazy people who would lock me in the cellar just for breaking something. So why would I be nervous when my whole life could change if I just control myself and don't do anything stupid? NOTHING STUPID. KEEP YOUR MOUTH SHUT.

Al backs her big Buick into a parking spot outside Friendly's. God, could she go any slower? I can't see them in the front windows. Maybe they aren't coming. That's happened before. The people say they're really, really interested in you and then they just don't show up.

"Come on, Andy, let's go meet them," Al says in her cheery voice. I hate her cheery voice.

"I don't think they're here."

"Don't worry. I spoke to them this morning."

We go inside and the place is filled. Great—so everybody in Friendly's is going to hear us talking about how I'm a poor little boy who needs a family. Why doesn't she just hang a sign on me—"Rotten Kid Thrown Away By His Parents. Anybody Want Him?"

"There they are," she says, "in the back."

Okay, Fleck, it's time to flip your hair off your face and smile. Show those dopey dimples.

"Andy, here are Jeff and . . ."

Oh God, I'm going to throw up. I know it. All over the table. Who would want a kid who barfs all over Friendly's? I wouldn't.

"Andy?"

"What?"

"I was introducing you to . . ."

"Oh yeah. Hi."

I need something to drink, fast. My mouth is as dry as dirt. Please let's sit down and order. "Al, I need a Coke, fast."

"How about Sprite? No caffeine."

"Anything, just fast."

We squeeze into a booth, and I'm stuck on the inside. I hate being on the inside like some little kid. I'm trapped. If I throw up now I'll be splashing everybody for sure.

"So," he says, "you play any sports?"

"Uh, not really." Wrong answer, Fleck. He looks like a jock type. "I mean, I could play sports. I just haven't gotten around to it yet. But I like sports a lot. You might say I'm a regular jock."

"Any sport in particular?"

Any sport? Think, Fleck. This isn't a toughie. What's the last thing you played? "Bowling, I like bowling. My father . . ." Shut up, don't mention him.

"Bowling, that's an interesting choice. I don't think they have that in our school. I was thinking of a sport more like baseball or soccer."

"Oh yeah, I love baseball, and soccer's my favorite."

"Andy hasn't had much chance to be on a team," Al says, "but he's very active."

The guy smiles and nods. His wife smiles and nods. They must want a baseball-hitting soccer-kicking super jock kind of kid. I guess I can be that.

"What other things do you like to do?" she asks me, and I take a glance at her because Al told me to look them in the eyes. She says adults like that. I didn't really notice before, but this woman looks a lot like Mom, only older. She's got the same brown hair and brown eyes.

Like to do? Is that what she asked? "I don't know. The usual stuff."

"You like playing video games," Al says.

I know she's trying to help, but sometimes social workers should just shut up. Parents don't like their kids playing videos. Any kid at The Home will tell you that—don't tell adults you like video games. They'll think you love splattering people all over the place with bullets and pulling their hearts out with your fingers.

"I don't play videos much anymore really, 'cause I guess I grew out of it. I like reading a lot now, and walking—I can walk for hours." Nice touch, Fleck. Who couldn't want a kid that likes to read and walk? And here comes the waitress with my burger and Sprite. Now we're rolling. What's this? They all ordered salads, even him. Can you imagine going to Friendly's and ordering a salad?

So I eat and nod, eat and nod. I don't even know what they're saying. Adults can talk on and on and the only thing you can do is smile and nod because who knows what they're saying even if you do hear them. I'm dripping ketchup all over the place, and I guess they don't notice because nobody's telling me to clean myself up. Except here comes the waitress with a stack of napkins big enough for the whole restaurant. She drops them down right in front of me. They all get a laugh out of that.

After the burger they order me a banana split. I'm going to bust open from all this food. But I keep eating away at the mounds of ice cream because Jeff and Whatever Her Name Is are laughing about my big appetite, so I can't stop now.

THREE

I'M GOING TO get a new family. I know it because I
wished for it on my lucky silver dollar that my mom gave
me. And then when I was shooting hoops with the guys,
I said that if my next shot went in I'd get this family. The
ball rolled around the rim and fell in, so that proved it.

José, he's my main buddy at The Home, he says something could go wrong, because what if there's some other
kid they're looking at and he was shooting hoops and hoping at the same time as me and his shot went in too? I said
that couldn't happen. Both shots couldn't go in so that other
kid must be lying. I know my shot went in and these two
parents are mine.

"Andy, would you please sit still," one of the counselors
says.

I can't I can't I can't. I hate sitting at these stupid little
tables doing stupid little drawings just because it's raining
out and they don't want us getting wet. I don't care about
rain. I want to get soaked and slide down Mud Hill with
José. Then I wouldn't be thinking about what I'm thinking
about, which I don't want to think about 'cause thinking
could jinx it.

God, where is she? Every time Al is supposed to come tell me something important she's late. It's almost one. She said she'd be here in the morning and this isn't morning anymore.

"Andy, do you need a time-out?"

No, I need parents, that's what. I don't want any more time-outs just because I can't sit still. I don't want to be drawing dopey pictures about My Favorite Animals, sitting at this cruddy old table with five other kids drawing stick figures instead of real animals. I need parents like Jeff and Whatever Her Name Is who like to go places and do stuff.

"Okay, Andy, you better—"

"No, wait. There she is in the parking lot, my social worker, so I have to see her."

I get to the door and open it and wait right there because I could get in big trouble if I stick even one toe outside without asking. I can't believe it—Al's stopping to talk to some lady. She knows everybody at The Home 'cause she's had other kids here before. You'd think she'd hurry since it's raining, but she stands there talking away for five whole minutes before heading for the door.

"Come on, Al, what'd they say? Are they going to take me?"

"Let me get inside, Andy." She squeezes past me and then goes over to talk to the head counselor, and he has to unlock the meeting room. So we go inside and Al takes off her jacket and sets down her pocketbook.

I can't stand it. I'll shake her arm off if she doesn't tell me. "Come on, Al—please!"

She's sort of grinning now, so I know she's teasing me. She wouldn't be doing that if they didn't want me.

"Yes," she finally says, "the Sizeracys called me today and said they would be very happy to start the formal visits with a certain young man named Andrew Fleck. If all goes well, you could move in before school starts."

I knew it! Wait till José hears this.

When you get a new foster family, the social worker just moves you right in. You don't even get to meet the people first. That's because foster homes are just temporary places where you stay while your social worker looks for an adoption family for you. Sometimes the foster parents start loving you so much they decide to adopt you. That never happened to me, but I did come close at my last foster home with a guy named Conner.

Adoption is different because it's forever. Once a family says they'll take you, then you go through a month or so of doing stuff with them to make sure you get along okay. Like with Jeff and Whatever Her . . . I mean, with Jeff and Laurie—that's her name. I don't know why I keep forgetting it. Anyway, they've taken me bowling and bike riding and kite flying. They took me to the Museum of Science in Boston, which has a giant movie screen about a hundred feet tall. I saw a movie about Africa, and even the little lion cubs looked big as elephants.

Today is supposed to be my last visit with Jeff and Laurie before I move in with them, and they gave me the choice of doing anything I wanted. I chose Six Flags.

José came here once and told me about it. It's the biggest amusement park I've ever seen, and I've been to lots of them. Dad used to take me every summer he wasn't locked up. We'd pack clothes and food for a week and head off in his old truck. We'd go to a different park every day and camp out in a field at night. Once we rode a roller coaster ten straight times without getting off. Then we got on the satellite and whirled around five times before I felt kind of dizzy and had to stop. My dad never got dizzy.

"So, what do you want to go on first?" Jeff asks as I'm taking a big bite of fried dough and chugging down my soda.

"Everything."

"That's inherently impossible," Laurie says with a little laugh.

I don't think she should be laughing at me like that. "Why not—we've got all afternoon before you dump me back at The Home, right? So we could do everything."

"I meant you can't do everything *first*. You'll have to choose something to start with."

"Yeah, whatever." She talks funny. I don't mean she has an accent or anything. It's just that lots of times she doesn't make sense. And she uses words I never even heard of before. I think she's trying to act smart. But it seems stupid to me to use big words when little words mean the same thing. "I want to go on the pirate's ship and in the fun house and then on the train thing that goes over your head . . ."

"The monorail," she says.

"Yeah, that, and the tilt-a-whirl and the snake and the bumper cars and then the roller coaster ten times."

"Well," Jeff says, "we better get started."

We went on everything, even the water ride where people almost died one time when their car flipped over. I wasn't scared though. Jeff sat next to me on everything. When the roller coaster or tilt-a-whirl turned a corner, he'd lean into me on purpose, flattening me against the side. It was pretty funny. I did that back at him on the next turn, but I couldn't push him much. Laurie came on some of the rides, and she usually had to sit one seat back because there wasn't room for all of us together. She didn't look like she was having much fun.

I want to go on the bumper cars one more time, but Jeff's shaking his head. "We've done just about every ride in the park," he says, "and it's getting dark. Time to head home . . . I mean take you back to The Home."

I don't want to go back there. I want to move in with them tonight. If I can't do that, then I want to go on the roller coaster again or the bumper cars.

"There is one more ride we could try," Laurie says. All right! She wants to stay too. But then she points to the giant glowing Ferris wheel about five stories high. "I want to go on that."

"Okay," Jeff says, "we'll make the Ferris wheel the last ride."

I can't believe it—the last ride on that? My dad never took me on the Ferris wheel. "No, Ferris wheels are dopey.

They just go around and 'round. They're slower than . . . than a clock. Ferris wheels are boring."

"They may be boring for you," Laurie says, "but not for me." She starts toward the ticket booth. "You coming?"

"No."

"Maybe I should stay with him," Jeff says.

"Andy's old enough to wait alone for a few minutes," she says, "aren't you?"

Of course I'm old enough. I stayed home alone all night sometimes when Mom was out. But I don't want to do that anymore. I don't like being alone. So I give her a shrug.

"Does that mean you can or can't, Andy?"

"It means I don't know."

"Well, you and Jeff went on dozens of rides today. I think you can wait on the bench for us now while we do the Ferris wheel, okay?"

It's not okay. It's just like what happened with my last foster dad, Conner. The wife gets all jealous when the guy wants to do stuff with me. Kids are supposed to do things with their dads, aren't they?

"We'll be back in ten minutes," Jeff says, and then she takes his hand and they head off.

I sit on the bench for a minute, which is pretty long for me to do nothing. I can hear Jeff yelling to me from the Ferris wheel, but I'm not going to look at him and wave. I'm going to walk the midway!

The first booth I come to there's a guy throwing darts at balloons. He's a lousy thrower, and it takes him ten dollars to win a big stuffed tiger for his little kid. Dad won me Ted, my stuffed bear, at a booth like this by knocking over some pins with a softball. That's the last thing he ever gave me. A couple days later he got caught robbing a store and was sent to jail. He wrote me letters every month, and he always asked how Ted was doing.

Thinking about Dad makes me feel pretty lousy. I mean, how come me—Andy Fleck—ended up with a father who's a thief and a mother who doesn't know how to be a mother? Why wasn't I born to Jeff and Laurie in the first place? That would have been perfect.

I figure they're probably done with the Ferris wheel, so I head back. On the way I see a men's room, so I run in there and out in about two seconds because it's pretty crummy.

When I reach the bench there's Laurie sitting alone, looking out over the crowd. "What's up?" I ask her.

She turns and looks at me like I'm a ghost who just popped out of the air.

"Andy," she says, "we've been searching all over for you. Where have you been?"

"I had to go."

"Go where?"

"I had to pee, okay? Is that a crime?"

"You couldn't hold it for ten minutes and wait here like I asked?"

"No way. I would have been peeing in my pants by that time. You wouldn't want a kid who did that, would you?"

"What I want," she says, "is . . ."

Is what? Why doesn't she know what she wants? I always know what I want.

"I just don't want any trouble, that's all."

I jump to my feet hearing that. That's exactly what my mom used to say about me—that I was always causing trouble. "I didn't do anything wrong. I wasn't causing trouble. I was peeing."

"Andy!" Jeff comes running out of the crowd and grabs me and hugs me like I've been lost for days. "Are you okay?"

"God, I'll never go pee again."

FOUR

TODAY'S THE DAY. The guys have been razzing me all morning. I don't blame them because I razzed Freddy, the kid who left last month. We put worms in his bed and threw his clothes out the window into the mud. At The Home, nobody can stand seeing somebody else getting out. It's like they're going and you're staying and how do you know, maybe you'll never leave?

Now I'm leaving. The guys said they're going to wait out front and tell my new family that I changed my mind or ran away or something. They don't know I told Jeff to come in the back door where I can see him from my window. No way I'm staying here another day.

Al gave me her usual lecture last night. She says I have to focus on my new family and forget all the bad stuff that happened with my old one. She means my mom disappearing for days when she was supposed to be home with me. And Dad, he wasn't any better at being a parent than he was robbing 7–11s, which was his favorite place to steal from. He was pretty good at breaking in, but sometimes he'd help himself to a snack along with the money, and the cops would catch him inside eating. Dad's a sucker for

Doritos, especially the barbecue ones. That's my favorite flavor too.

Al says I don't have to forget my parents, just the stuff they did to me—and didn't do, like actually take care of me. She says I'd suffered from Neglect for almost my whole life, and I need to clear my mind of the past so I'll be ready for a new family. She says that my mom and dad actually did me a favor giving me up to the state, since they couldn't be proper parents. Now it's up to me to take advantage of Opportunity. Okay, I'll give Opportunity a try. I don't have any choice anyway. I sure don't want to live in The Home forever. I need some parents.

And this time I picked them! Al wasn't sure at first that they were right for me. She said they never had a kid before and they were actually looking for a six year old. But I kept bugging her to call them back because I could tell at the adoption party that they were interested. I'm interested in them too. He always wants to do stuff with me, like play sports and ride bikes. And she smells good, like the lilacs growing outside my window at my last foster home. José says I better watch out. He says people who take twelve year olds want them to do tons of yard work. He knows that for a fact. If that's true, they're going to be in for a surprise with me. This kid doesn't work for nothing.

I asked José to play cards with me until they came, but he said he had something to do. Then he stuck his hand out for me to shake, and that was weird because we never did that before. And it wasn't his good left hand he was sticking out. It was his right hand that hangs off his elbow, which is how he was born. He never let anybody touch it before, not even me. But this time he pulled up his shirt-sleeve and stuck out his little hand and I shook it. Then he ran out of my room and was gone.

God, this place stinks. It's like they shoot Lysol out with a firehose to clean the halls. Then they nail shut the windows so you can't breathe. But what do I care? This is my last day at The Home.

Oh man, there's Jeff coming across the parking lot, and The Worm's hanging on him already. That kid will do anything to get a family. I'm outta here.

Before I can get to the back door Jeff's coming down the hallway. "Hey, kiddo," he says, "how you doing?"

Kiddo? My name's Andy. I guess he's trying to be friendly. "I'm okay. What'd The Worm want?"

"The Worm?"

"Yeah, the kid outside hanging on you."

"He was just helping me find you."

"He probably asked you to take him home with you, didn't he? He asks everybody who comes in here."

"And nobody takes him?"

Boy, he doesn't know The Worm. "The Worm's got lots of problems, like . . . he wets his bed and stutters. I'm prac-tically the only one who plays with him."

"That's nice of you."

It feels strange being called "nice." Most people say I'm

obnoxious, and I really am lots of times. It's not that I try to be obnoxious. Most of the time I don't even know I'm being obnoxious until someone tells me.

"Okay," he says, "whom do we check out with?"

"They said I can just leave because you signed all the papers before. They're all busy in the time-out room holding down Lubby."

"Who's that?"

I shape the air into an outline of a huge body, which is the only way to describe Lubby. "He's, like, 250 pounds, and when he flips out it takes all of the Hulks to hold him."

"The Hulks?"

"Yeah, the counselors. We call them the Hulks 'cause they're all big like the wrestlers on TV."

We head off and he's picking his way around the mattresses, which are in the hallway because it's room-cleaning day. Me, I'm walking right across them with my muddy sneakers. The guys are going to know I left. At the door Jeff holds up my bag. "Is this all you have?"

What, does he think I don't own anything? "No way. Sammy's carrying the rest out to the car."

"Who's Sammy?"

"He's a janitor sort of guy. He's kind of on the dumb side, you know, 'cause he got dropped on his head when he was being born. So he'll do whatever you tell him, even if he's not supposed to."

"And you got him to carry your stuff out so you wouldn't have to?"

"Yeah, pretty smart, huh?"

He holds the plastic bag out to me. What's he up to? "I'm not carrying that."

He drops the bag to the floor. "Then I guess your things stay here, for The Worm or one of the other boys."

He's got me this time. I couldn't stand to have another kid pawing through my stuff.

At the car, my things are stacked by the trunk. Sammy is walking away, pulling his red wagon behind him. "Hey, Sammy!" I yell to him, and he stops and turns around slowly. Sammy never does anything fast. "See ya, wouldn't want to be ya." He grins and waves. I'm not going to miss much at The Home, but I'll miss Sammy and José.

Jeff opens the trunk and begins loading. I've got bags of shirts and sweaters that I never wear because they came from Goodwill. I've got a dozen board games and about the same number of books. There are boxes full of metal, wires, screws, and bolts—I can't remember what they came from. Sammy used to collect old things from trash bins and let me take them apart.

Jeff holds up a busted circuit board. "What is all of this anyway?"

"I don't know. I just take things apart. I don't memorize every little piece."

"You know how to put things back together?"

"Naw, that would be like work, and I don't do work." He laughs like I'm kidding and then stuffs my big black trash bag into the side of the trunk. "Hey, don't crush that."

"What's in here?" he asks.

"It's my stuffed animals. I used to have a ton more, but Weird Joan took one away every time I said a swear."

"Who's Weird Joan?"

How could he not know about her? Didn't he read my file? "She was my third foster mother. She was the worst. One time she hit my rabbit so hard the stuffing popped out of him. She wouldn't even give me a needle to sew him up."

"Sounds like she was pretty angry at you."

"I was pretty angry at *her*." He starts to shut the trunk, and suddenly I remember Ted. "Hold on." I dig in the trunk and pull Ted from the black bag. I figure I might as well let Jeff know right away the way things stand. "Nobody beats up one of my animals and gets away with it."

He nods like he understands. "So," he says as we climb into the car, "what did you do to get back at Weird Joan?"

Yeah, like I'm really going to tell him. "Wouldn't you like to know?"

Good-bye Hulks and crazy shrinks and cooks who can't even make toast without burning it. Good-bye to toilets that don't flush and ratty mattresses and slime-green walls. Good-bye to The Home, hope to never see you again.

The guys are on the field getting up a game of flag football. "Hey—I'm going!" They don't hear me yelling from the car, or at least they don't look up as we go by. I guess I never waved to anybody leaving either.

"We have about an hour's ride," Jeff says as we pull out onto the main road. "How about we play a game to pass the time?"

A car game? Like alphabet, or colors? God, kill me now. "What kind of game?"

"I was thinking of a guessing game. I'll ask you questions, such as, What's your favorite kind of fruit? And then I'll try to guess it."

Sounds pretty lame, but what the heck? I got an hour with nothing to do. So I reach around to the backseat to get my notebook from my backpack. "I can write my answers on this, so I won't cheat."

"I'm not worried that you'll cheat."

"You're not? I am."

"Oh, okay. Ready? What's your favorite fruit?"

That's easy. I cover the paper with my hand and write *apple*.

"Banana," he says. Then he guesses apple. "All right, your favorite sport?" I write down *baseball* 'cause I know he loves the Red Sox, and that's what he guesses right away. We go through the different categories pretty fast: The vegetable I hate the most—squash. My favorite TV show—*The Simpsons*. My favorite flavor—cherry. Favorite boy's name other than my own—Frank. The name I'd want if I'd been born a girl—Kelly.

"That's a nice name," he says.

"It's my aunt's name—one of them, anyway. I mean one of my aunts, not one of her names."

"And Frank? Why is that your favorite?"

This is weird. Doesn't he even know my dad's name? He must have gotten all the papers from Al. Dad's name had to be in there, unless it got erased. "Frank's my father's name—my *old* father, I mean, but he's really not old. He's probably younger than you. What are you, like forty?"

"I was forty four years ago."

"I think he's thirty-four now—my old dad, I mean. It sounds stupid calling him that, since you're older."

"How about calling him your *first* dad?"

"Okay, then that makes you my *last* dad." The words just pop out of my mouth. Could Jeff really be the last dad I ever have to get used to?

He turns away as if checking the traffic over his left shoulder. Maybe he's going to cry and doesn't want me to see. He probably never had anybody call him Dad before.

"My first dad took me up in a helicopter once, and the pilot passed out from being sick. Dad was in the backseat, and he told me to pull back on this lever thing, and I did that, which kept us from crashing. Another time we got lost in a canoe on this big lake. I forget which one. It sounded like some Indian . . ."

"The Quabbin Reservoir?"

"Yeah, that's it. We got lost and all we had to drink was Bud, so we downed a six-pack and got pretty drunk."

"Hmmm," Jeff says. I guess he doesn't know what to say about beer drinking.

"I've had lots of adventures," I tell him so he knows who he's dealing with. I'm not one of those kids who sits at home watching TV all the time. I want to do stuff. "Like, with Conner . . ."

"Who's that?"

"My last foster dad. He took me deep-sea fishing one

time in the ocean, and he threw up 'cause the boat was rocking so much, but I didn't. And then Richard—no, wait, it was Joe, yeah Joe—he took me skiing somewhere in New Hampshire, except I didn't want to ski. I wanted to snowboard. So I did and the first time I went all the way down the hill. They never had anybody do that before, not the first time."

"Sounds like you're a pretty good athlete. How come you haven't gone out for any sports?"

Because I have this problem with people telling me what to do, that's why. But I can't say that, so I'll tell him what Al says. "I've moved so many times in the last two years that I haven't been in any school long enough to go out for anything."

"It must be tough moving so often."

"Yeah, but I'm used to it."

"Can you get used to living in one place now?"

I know what he means—with him and Laurie. I'm sure I could get used to them, and I want to. But I've never gotten anything I really wanted, so why should I think my luck will change now? When you're a foster kid you learn not to hope for anything much. Jeff's still driving along waiting for my answer, but I don't have one.

FIVE

WE'VE BEEN DRIVING for almost an hour, so we must be getting close to my new house. Al wanted them to bring me out here for a visit first, but I said no. I didn't want to see it until the day I was absolutely definitely moving in. José visited two houses he was supposed to move into, and then he never did. I didn't want that happening to me.

Boy, what a neighborhood! Some of these places look like those mansions you see on TV that the rich and famous live in. I'd like to be rich and famous someday. But if I could only be one or the other, I'd choose rich.

There's a house with a big gate across the driveway. Maybe that's going to be mine. "Is that it?"

He laughs and keeps on driving, so I guess not. The next house has a pool on the side. I'd be out there all summer doing cannonballs. "How about that one?"

"No, not quite," he says. Right by it is a house that has big columns in the front, like at the White House. "No, not that one either," he says before I even ask. We turn down a few more streets, and the houses get a lot smaller. Suddenly he pulls into a driveway and stops. I guess this is it. The house is short and white and kind of small. But there are Christmas-type trees all over the place, and other kinds I don't know the names of. Jeff will have to teach me.

"This is our little home," he says.

He sounds kind of embarrassed after all the castles we've been passing. But I don't care. I'm not used to fancy houses anyway. I'd probably just end up breaking expensive stuff. We leave my things in the trunk, and he leads me up the steps and around the walk to the front door. As soon as we get inside, Laurie calls to us from somewhere, "I'm baking cookies in here, in case anyone's hungry."

Jeff points me to the kitchen, and there she is. She looks dopey now, not like Mom at all. Her hair is pulled back, and she's wearing an apron that has foreign words on it. Mom never wore an apron. "I saved this for you," she says and holds out a bowl of dough.

I put my hands behind my back. "I don't like cookies. I mean, I like them, but the sugar gets me hyper."

"That's okay," Jeff says and sticks his finger in the bowl to scoop up some of the dough. "I can eat all the cookies Laurie can make, no problem."

There's a huge black ant crawling across the tile floor. Should I step on it? I better not. I think they're big animal rights people since they wouldn't take me to the circus because they said the elephants aren't treated very well.

"Come on," he says, "it's too hot to stand around in the kitchen. I'll show you the backyard, and we can look for Tiger."

A tiger? Who's he kidding? "You don't have a tiger."

"No, that's our cat. She has the coloring of a tiger, and she hunts like one, so that's her name."

I follow him through the porch and out onto the back deck. Wow! The yard is big enough for a whole football game. There are millions of trees for climbing and swinging on a tire and making a fort. "All of this is yours?"

"Yep, back to the wetlands, it's all ours."

Does he mean mine too? Sure, why wouldn't he? I'm the kid of the house now, so this is my yard. Boy, the grass is high. Maybe José was right—they got me to mow the lawn.

We head over to the woodpile, and there's Tiger sitting with a dead mouse between her front paws. Its feet are sticking straight up. Tiger's swatting at the mouse and then pouncing on it as if it's still alive. Jeff pulls her away and holds her out toward me. Since I had Orange I know how to meet a strange cat. You stick your finger slowly to its nose so it can smell you—don't make any sudden moves or it might get scared and bite. Tiger sniffs my hand, and then she rubs her face on it!

"I had a cat once, twice as big as this one."

"What happened to her?"

"It was a 'him.' I named him Orange."

"What happened to Orange?"

"He ran off. I think he knew Mom and Dad didn't really want him. They only got him for me."

Jeff sets Tiger on the ground and starts off across the yard, so I follow him. If I jump a little I can put my feet down exactly in his footprints. Nobody would know there

were two people walking in the grass. Dad taught me this.
He said it might come in useful for me to know someday.
At the edge of the yard, Jeff spins around like he's trying
to catch me at something wrong. "What? I'm not doing
anything."

"I didn't say you were."

He gets this little shovel from the garage, and we go back
to the woodpile to scoop up the dead mouse. "I could've just
picked it up in my hands, you know."

"A mouse can carry ticks," he says, "and certain ticks
cause Lyme disease. So it's safer not to touch it."

He carries the mouse behind the fence and lifts the
edge of an overturned bucket. I can't believe it—there are
all kinds of half-eaten things under there. "What is this?"

"I call it Tiger's Death Pail. Even with two bells on, she's fast enough to catch anything that moves in the yard."

I grab a stick from the ground and poke at the skin of a snake that looks like leather and a big lump of feathers covered with red ants. Jeff says this was a female pheasant. Tiger's awesome. And now she's mine.

It took us three trips to unload the car. I never ever brought this much stuff with me to a new home before.

Laurie is watching me now from the doorway of my room. She thinks I'm not doing anything 'cause I'm lying on my bed with my hands behind my head, and my junk is still spread all over the floor. What I'm doing is deciding, like which posters to hang on the wall and where to put my desk and whether to push my bed under the window. For about the hundredth time she asks me if I need help. I don't need any help. I've got all the time in the world.

"You sure?" she says.

Why doesn't she stop bugging me? "Yeah, I'm really, really, really sure, okay? I have to put my stuff away myself 'cause then I'll know where everything is when I need it."

She finally gets the hint and closes the door behind her. It's spooky all of a sudden, being alone in a room of my own like this, in a house where I've never been before. In my foster homes I usually had to share with some other kid who acted even dopier than me. The last time I had a room all my own was with Mom. That was great, except for when she went out at night and left me home. Then I wished I had an older brother living there or even a stupid little brother—anybody so I wouldn't have to stay alone. It was scary. I could hear stuff going on in the apartment next door that I didn't want to think about. Sometimes I'd hear somebody on the fire escape outside or walking around in the halls. I locked up every window in the apartment as soon as she left. Then I set up my stuffed animals around the edge of my bed. I pretended they were lookouts, like armed bears. I know that sounds pretty dumb, but I felt better anyway.

I read to keep myself awake. I went through all of Mark Twain's books, starting with *Life on the Mississippi*. Then I found Douglas Adams's *Hitchhiker* series at the library and read all of them. Whenever I started falling asleep, I pricked my finger with a pin.

Mom usually got home around midnight. She never came in to say good night, and I didn't really want her to because I knew she'd stink of beer. That smell is enough to make you heave, especially when it's on your mother.

In the mornings I'd check on her and she always looked dead. Sometimes I held a little mirror to her mouth to see if it fogged up, meaning that she was breathing. I saw that on TV once. I don't know what I would have done if she wasn't breathing—probably jumped out of my skin like Tom and Huck did when they saw a dead man. But I couldn't go to school not knowing if she was alive.

On my tenth birthday I found a small package with my name on it lying on the floor under the mail slot. I opened it and out fell a pen with a note from Dad saying, "Be careful how you use this." I couldn't figure that out. I mean,

Dad isn't the sort of guy who cares about writing, and how dangerous can a pen be? Anyway, I clicked the thing a few times and out popped a three-inch knife blade! Now that sounded like Dad. When I took it to school to show my friends, old Mr. Kaiser, the hall monitor, caught me. That guy must have been a hundred years old, but he still saw every little thing a kid did wrong. He dragged me down to the principal's, and I got suspended for bringing a birthday present to school!

It took them awhile to wake Mom up—she can sleep through anything. They didn't believe me that she was home because they kept calling and calling and she didn't answer. They finally sent a cop car around and rang the buzzer until she got up. She came to school at noon to get me. On the way home she gave me this lecture about how I needed to be more responsible for myself, and when was I going to learn to stay out of trouble? That was strange—I mean, I should have been lecturing her, right?

She dropped me off at the apartment and took off to who knows where. It wasn't right that she got to go out again and I had to stay in just because Dad sent me the knife. So I caught the bus downtown and hung around Fanueil Market-place for a while. That's this old warehouse area in Boston that's been turned into fancy shops. All the kids who skip school go there 'cause you can lose yourself in the crowds. Even if the cops see you they figure you're just some kid from out of state on vacation, so they don't bust you.

When it got late that afternoon, I checked all my pockets and couldn't find a cent. I'd blown my last quarter skiing at the Virtual Reality place. I didn't have any money left to take the bus home, and I sure wasn't going to walk three miles. I asked some people for the dollar I needed, but they acted like I was invisible. I guess that's how beggars feel when they stick their hand out and people just walk by. One guy told me to get a job delivering newspapers. Adults can be really annoying. I needed a dollar *now*. Anyway, I decided to get my own money, and that's when I got caught with my hand in the old guy's pocket. The cop who took me in was pretty nice. He bought me an ice cream on the way to the station. But I still wouldn't tell him where I lived or what my name was. Finally he bribed me with a strawberry frappé and some fries, so I said my name was Oliver Twist. He actually wrote this down! I guess he doesn't read much. Boy was he mad when he found out I was lying.

I never went home again. It took the social worker a whole day to track down Mom. Dad was easier to find, being in jail. A couple of months went by while the social workers tried to get things straightened out so I could go back home. Al says Mom and Dad both had plenty of chances to be proper parents, but they didn't want to change. I guess they were just too busy to have a kid like me around anymore.

I'm majorly thirsty. At The Home you have to wait until snack time to get something to drink, but not here. I just run out of my bedroom and down the hall in my socks and slide into the living room. "Help! Quick! I'm dying of thirst. I need something to drink."

Jeff gets up from the couch. Laurie doesn't look too

happy. Maybe I interrupted them sucking lips. God, I'm glad I didn't see that. "Come on, hurry. I'm practically dying!"

"Let's see what we have," he says and sticks his head into the refrigerator. "Diet Coke, milk, orange juice, cider, root beer."

"I'll take beer." He laughs like I'm kidding. "I've had beer before."

"I know. You told me in the car."

"Even before that. My dad said he put it in my bottle when I was a baby. That's the only way I'd go to sleep."

I don't think he likes hearing about Dad because he gets this strange look on his face, like he's got wicked gas. Then he uncaps a root beer and hands it to me. "Enjoy your beer," he says. Very funny.

SIX

THIS IS THE life! After I unpacked my things, I said, "I think I'll go down to the playroom for a while," and here I am. Just me. At The Home there'd be five guys fooling around in a room like this and a couple of Hulks watching. Here I can lie out on the couch like I own the place. I do sort of own it—at least I will if they actually adopt me.

It doesn't really feel like a basement because it's only half underground. There's a big window to the backyard, and I can look straight out at the red squirrels jumping through the grass. I've only seen gray squirrels in the city. Jeff said woodchucks live back there and pheasants, which I've never seen in my life except the one under Tiger's Death Pail, so that doesn't count. He said that deeper in the woods deer live. I'm going to watch for everything.

My new parents sure must read a lot. There's probably a thousand books on the shelves, and that's just in this room. I'm going to read every one of them and I'm going to know everything in them forever because I don't forget stuff. If I hear a song once I can sing it back months later. I can remember what happened in a book and who the characters are even if it was a couple years ago that I read it.

Some of their books look wicked dull, like *How We Die* and *The Mushroom Handbook*. Who would read them? But they got some cool ones too, like *Zolar's Book of Forbidden Knowledge* and *King Arthur's Knights*. I think I'm going to start with *Been Down So Long It Looks Up to Me*. I don't know what that means, but there's this sexy woman on the front, and that's for me. They don't know enough to hide books like that. They never had a twelve year old in the house before, that's for sure.

Laurie didn't even come to pick me up from The Home today. I don't really care 'cause I got to talk to Jeff alone. I thought he was going to cry when I said he could be my *last* dad. My social worker said they really wanted a kid and couldn't have one of their own. I guess they were so desperate that they're happy even to get me!

Anytime I want anything from Jeff, I'll just haul out the old "Daddy" routine. "Hey, Dad, can you buy me a new bike, Dad? Please . . . Daddy."

Got to eat, got to eat, got to eat. It must be lunchtime.

I wonder what kind of food they have in a house like this. Some places they feed you queer stuff like thick greasy salamis or hot chili or big pots of garbage soup. I'm not making that up. Garbage soup is a huge pot of all the leftovers in the refrigerator, and it tastes like garbage too. That was Weird Joan's special meal when she wanted to make me throw up. At The Home they just gave us chicken and hamburgers—chicken one night, hamburgers the next. I think it's because they're both cheap.

I go upstairs to the kitchen, and Laurie is pulling out all sorts of junk from the refrigerator. "Let's see," she says, "what would you like for lunch? We have seafood salad, bagels and cream cheese, some leftover pasta, boiled ham."

No, no, no, especially the ham. I'm not eating meat ever again.

"There's hummus—I could make . . ."

"What's that?"

"Hummus is ground up chickpeas . . ."

"Chick pee?"

"Chickpeas—P-E-A-S."

That sounds terrible. Why would anybody eat ground up chickpeas? What are they anyway?

"There's soup in the cabinet, split pea—P-E-A—and probably some clam chowder."

This woman really needs help. I better take control of the lunch situation right now or they'll try to shove that hummus down my throat every day. "You know how to make a greasy cheese?"

"I don't think I do."

Looks like I have to teach another one. I grab the bread off the counter and open the refrigerator to get the butter, but where's the Velveeta? "No Velveeta?"

"I know it's hard to believe, but we've been getting along without it."

I think she's trying to be funny, but I don't see the joke in not having Velveeta in the house. "What else you got?"

"There's Muenster."

"Monster?"

She pulls a plastic bag from the refrigerator and holds it up. "Muenster—it's a fairly bland kind of cheese."

"Blond?"

"Bland—that means mild, without a strong taste."

I take a sniff of the bag, and it doesn't smell much at all. "Okay, all you do is put about a half inch of cheese in the bread, and then you nuke some butter and pour it on the sandwich before frying it."

"Sounds like it could kill you instantly—from the cholesterol."

"Not me." I cut off half a stick of butter and drop it in a bowl for microwaving. "I got the lowest cholesterol of anybody ever tested at The Home—I think it was fifty, or something like that. They give you a physical when you go in there and the doctor said I'm perfect, except I'm too skinny. I could eat ten greasy cheeses and still not gain any weight. And I get these rashes sometimes, which no-body knows what causes that. It's a medical mystery." The microwave beeps and I take out the bowl of liquid butter. I spoon it on either side of the sandwich to soak the bread. "Okay, you can fry this. Then when you flip it over, pour on more butter." She does as I tell her, no questions asked. That's the way I like it. "And of course, I got these head problems—you know about them, right?"

"I'm not sure I do," she says.

"Well, that's what I take the Ritalin and Depakote for. If my brain was working right, I wouldn't need the meds."

She flips the sandwich onto a plate, and I take a test bite. Not bad, for a rookie greasy cheese maker.

"You think the medicines help you?"

"Naw, I can't tell the difference. When I miss my meds, people always say, 'You're acting like a different boy today, Andy.' But to me, I seem like myself all the time."

"Well, Alison told us they help you concentrate, so we want to remember for you to take them."

She starts to clean up the dishes, and that's when it's time for me to scram, before she asks me to help.

Not long after lunch I'm looking out of my bedroom window at some bluejays chasing each other in the front yard. I think they're fighting over a worm in the grass, but maybe they're just play-fighting, like José and I do. It's hard to tell with birds and kids when they're serious. Sometimes José and I started out play-fighting and then got mad at each other. It usually ended up with him sitting on my chest until I called him José the Great.

So I'm looking out of my window and there comes Al down the street in her green Buick. I threw up in that car the first time she took me to an adoption party. She didn't act very surprised when I did. She just pulled some paper towels from under her seat and cleaned up. I guess lots of kids throw up when they're looking for a family.

I don't know why Al's showing up the first day I'm here. I haven't done anything wrong yet. Now's the time for me to hide behind the sofa in the living room and spy on them.

In a minute she rings the bell and then comes in like she's been invited. That's Al for you. She goes right to the dining-room table and spreads out her papers for Jeff and

Laurie. "Just a few things to sign," she says. "It's all formali-
ties. You're acknowledging that you're taking possession of
Andy—"

Wait a minute—possession? What am I, some kind of
stray dog? Nobody owns me.

"—and you'll monitor his medical and dental needs,
and you agree to monthly visits by me to make sure everything's going fine. If it is, we can finalize the adoption in
about six months." She looks around, and I have to duck
back to my hiding spot behind the sofa. "Where is Andy,
by the way? He hasn't run off yet, has he?" She laughs like
she's making a joke, but she knows I've run away before.

"I'm here," I call out from the living room. "I was listening to everything you said."

Al leans around the dining-room wall. "Listen all you
want, Andy. You know I don't keep secrets from you."

Right, like she really told me Weird Joan was weird and
Dumb Donald was dumb before she put me with them.

"And signing this part," Al says, "means that you accept
the state payment of $15.47 per day for Andy. That's the
rate for children eleven and over."

So that's what I'm worth—$15.47 a day. Not bad. Maybe
that's why they're taking me. Why else would anyone want
a twelve year old?

This sure isn't Boston. I can't even see another house
from the backyard. These people must be loaded if they
own this many trees. I told Al I wanted a rich family this
time, but I never thought one would take me. I bet the

trees are a hundred feet high. I'm going to climb the tallest one and look over the whole world.

"Andy, are you out there? I have to leave now."

Al knows I'm hiding from her. We do this every time I go to a new house. She calls me and I don't answer, so she doesn't know if I've run away or not. She can't go without knowing I'm all right, so she has to come looking for me. She's muttering about how she's got other boys to take care of and when she turns her back, I spring on her from behind a tree— "Boo!"

"Okay, you scared me, Andy," she says, but she doesn't laugh and rub my head like usual. She's getting serious on me, which means I'm in for one of her lectures. "You know, you've been through a lot of families in the last two years."

"Yeah, I know."

"It's got to stop some time. You can't keep busting out of places. You're going to run out of chances."

"You mean this is my last chance?"

"I didn't say that. I'm just saying it's a real good chance for you."

She puts her hand up for a high five, like I taught her, and I give her a soft five, which she taught me after I almost broke her finger one time.

"I know we rushed the visiting stage a little this time, but that's because school starts on Thursday, and we wanted you settled. You did some good work on your behavior at The Home. That's why we placed you so fast."

"Fast? I went to like fifteen adoption parties before somebody took me."

"It was only five, and that's not many for a twelve year old. Now, are you going to try a little harder here to make things work out for yourself?"

"I guess."

Al finally smiles and messes up my hair like old times. Then I follow her inside the back door, through the side porch, and into the living room where Jeff and Laurie are standing pretending they haven't been watching us. "I think that's everything," Al says to them, and I'm hoping she'll forget my meds. But then she opens her pocketbook and pulls out two pill bottles. "Here are Andy's Ritalin and Depakote. He takes two white ones at breakfast and two orange at dinner, right, Andy?"

Yeah, sure, except when I tongue them and spit them out later. Those pills don't do anything except keep me short. How am I supposed to grow up like everybody tells me to when I'm taking all this stuff?

"You know the Ritalin helps you focus, Andy, and the Depakote helps your behavior, so you're going to help remember to take them, aren't you?"

Oh yeah, and I'll grow wings and fly away too. If Jeff and Laurie don't remember, that's their fault. I'm not doing their job for them.

Al moves closer to the door. You can tell she wants to get out of here fast. She hates working Saturdays. "You have the after-hours number to call if there's any problem." She whispers this last part to them, as if I don't know about the Parents' Panic Number. I called it myself once when Joan and Donald tried to lock me in the cellar. 1-800-SCREWUU—that's how I remember it.

Jeff opens the screen door and they all go out on the front steps to talk some more about me. I'm alone again, which is hard to get used to. At The Home they watch you every second in case you go ballistic and punch out the walls. They even took the doors off the toilets so you couldn't hide in there.

There's not much in this living room for a kid, that's for sure. No Sega, no beanbag chair, no super-sized TV, no nothing. There's wooden elephants all over the place and fancy golden plates on the wall and dumb paintings that look like somebody threw up different colors. Everything in the room has probably been nailed to the same place for years. They'll jump through the roof when I break something. I'm spending my time in the playroom. I'll have to work on Jeff to get me a TV down there.

There goes the phone ringing—boy, it's loud. They must be deaf if they can't hear it. They're just standing out there talking, talking, talking. Maybe they have an answering machine. I don't care. I'm not picking it up. I didn't come here to be a slave.

They never had a foster kid before, I can tell that. Laurie left her pocketbook sitting on the table. Her wallet is sticking out on top. She doesn't know better than to leave money lying around. But Al must have told them I take things sometimes. So why did she leave her pocketbook right out in the open? Maybe she doesn't want me. Maybe it was

Jeff's idea to get me, and she's trying to trap me into taking something so he'll kick me out. I'll show her—I'm not going to steal a thing.

Al probably told them about the Morrisseys' old cat falling out of the window, too. She always tells new parents everything. I didn't do it on purpose. I was just crawling out on the roof to cool off after we had this big argument. I was thinking about jumping off the roof myself and running away. Then I saw the cat come out through the window I'd left open. I tried to grab her but she dove away from me and fell to the ground. It wasn't my fault she got killed. Cats are supposed to land on their feet. I would never hurt a cat. Why wouldn't anybody believe me?

I'm going to watch after Tiger and make sure nothing happens to her. I love Tiger, and she's going to love me.

SEVEN

AL GUNS HER Green Monster up the street and hits the horn three times, which is her good-bye signal to me. She's gone. Now what?

"Well, Andy," Jeff says as he comes in the door, "what would you like to do this afternoon?"

How should I know? Parents almost never ask me what I want. "You live here. You're supposed to know what to do."

"How about we go to Walden Pond?" he says.

"What's that?"

"It's a famous lake nearby here where—"

"I thought you said it was a pond."

"It's called a pond, but it's the size of a lake. Henry David Thoreau wrote a famous book about living by himself in the woods at Walden. Maybe you've heard of him."

"Not really."

"Well, he wasn't as alone as he let on. In the winter, ice cutters would come from Boston to chop out big chunks from the pond. And in the summer, he used to walk into town and steal pies off the windowsills where the women put them to cool."

Stealing pies, that sounds kind of interesting. "What kind of pies?"

"I don't know—blueberry, apple, rhubarb, all kinds."

"Okay, I'll go."

"Great," he says. "Put your swim trunks on. How soon can you be ready, Laurie?"

She comes in from the kitchen, wiping her hands on her apron. "You two go. I just put the rest of the cookies in the oven and I have to wait for the call from Walpole."

Walpole? That's a dumb name. "Who's that?"

"It's a place—a prison."

Cool. "You know somebody doing time?"

"I don't really know him," she says. "I interviewed him for a television report that's going to be on tonight. Remember, I told you I work for channel 7?"

"I know somebody doing time. Maybe you could put him on your show too."

Imagine that, my dad on TV. He'd be a star!

It's hot and crowded at this place called Walden Pond. If that guy Thoreau came here to get away from people, like Jeff says, it must have been a million years ago. He's heading across the beach like he knows where he's going, so I'll just follow along. But it's boring walking through sand. Why do adults do everything the boring way? There's a neat stone wall to hop up on. That's where I'm walking.

"Not much of a day for lying in the sun," he says when we get to the far end of the beach. The wind is whipping up little swirls in the sand, like miniature tornadoes, and he uses our sneakers to hold down the ends of our blanket. We're away from most everybody over here, and I wonder if that's because he doesn't want to be seen with me. Maybe he doesn't want people to think I'm his kid.

"You're not supposed to get a tan," I tell him, "'cause that gives you cancer. Didn't you know that?"

Who wants to lie around anyway? I throw off my shirt and then blast off into the water! It feels awesome—like a huge balloon full of cold water dropping on my head. What's he doing, walking in like a wimp? "Come on, it's warm. Don't you even know how to dive in?" I splash a little and then get closer and closer until I spray him all over. He puffs himself up like some kind of monster, and I have to dive under to get away from him.

When I come up for air, he's standing only a few feet away. "Oh shhh . . . oot!" That's good, Fleck, watch your swears. This is just the first day. You got to be on your best behavior. It's time to impress him. "I have a horse, you know, but I don't come with a horse. I used to come with a bird, but I don't now."

"Why's that?" he says.

"I starved him."

"You mean you didn't feed your bird on purpose so he'd die?"

"No, I just forgot to." That's the truth.

"What about the horse?"

"My dad gave him to me. My aunt's keeping him until I'm old enough."

"Oh really?"

He looks at me like he doesn't believe me. You can tell when adults don't believe you—they always say something like, "Oh really?" I don't care if he believes me. I could have had a horse. Dad said he would buy me one someday.

I know—I'll show him my underwater handstand. Dive! Dive! Perfect, Fleck. Grab some sand to anchor yourself, legs straight up—what's going on? He's touching my foot. My legs crash to the water and I burst into the air again. "What'd you do that for?"

"I was just fooling with you," he says.

Okay, don't get excited. Maybe he was just fooling and didn't mean anything by it. Just because one of mom's boyfriends touched you where he shouldn't have doesn't mean Jeff would. He was probably just tickling.

I glide toward him, my mouth just above the water. I feel like a shark going in for the kill. "You can't tickle worth anything, I bet. You're probably the worst tickler in the world."

"I can tickle with the best of them," he says, "if I want to."

"I think you're a tickling wimp."

"Hey, look at that dog swimming," he says, pointing behind me.

When I stand up to see, he grabs me in a bear hug from behind and tickles my stomach. I'm thrashing around and shouting so much the whole beach is looking at us. "They think you're touching me under the water." That's what I tell him, and he lets go. He looks scared all of a sudden, and I know I've hit on something. José says the first thing you have to do in a new family is find out what scares the parents. It's only the first day and I already know that about Jeff—he's scared that I might say he's touching me. "I could make them think you're doing it, if I wanted to."

He's staring at me now like he can't believe what I'm saying. "Why would you want to?"

Okay, he's got me there. Why would I? Time to dive again.

Later, after we dry off and head back to the parking lot, I figure it's time to see how much Al told them about me. "So, you know I'm obnoxious, right?"

He keeps walking as if I'm asking a normal question, like, "You know I'm part Irish, right?" Al told me once that "obnoxious" was the word that a lot of parents used about me, and I should try to figure out why. I did think about it for maybe ten seconds, and I couldn't come up with a reason except that I really am obnoxious sometimes. It's not that I try to be. And I don't want to be. I'm not sure if I was born obnoxious or just grew up that way because of Mom and Dad. All I know is that people call me obnoxious. So if that's the way I am, my new parents better know it right off. If they still want me, then fine.

"I know you do things at times that annoy people," Jeff says, "if that's what you mean."

"I mean I'm obnoxious. And another thing, everything always goes wrong when I'm around."

We get to the top of this huge stone staircase and cross the street to the parking lot. "We've been having a good day," he says, "right?"

"Yeah, but it isn't over yet."

"I bet if you think about it you could come up with a lot of things that have gone right for you."

Boy is he wrong. I've already thought about it. "I wasn't even born right."

"What do you mean?"

"I came out the wrong way."

"You mean feet first?"

"Yeah, and I almost suffocated because my head got stuck."

"Who told you that?"

"My mom. She always tells people I hurt like hell coming out—sorry, that's what *she* said, not me. She said it was like trying to pop a bowling ball out of her."

The parking lot is filled with a lot more cars than when we got here, and he doesn't know where he left the Saab. Fleck to the rescue! I run up one row and down the next, jump in the air a few times to see all around . . . and there it is. "Over here! I found it." Boy was he lost. It's a good thing he has me or he would have been looking for hours.

He opens the door to the car and we sit on either side, wiping the sand from our feet. "A lot of kids come out breech," he says. "You're not the only one."

Breech—that's the word Mom used too. "Whatever it's called, I came out wrong."

EIGHT

SHE'S ON TV. I can't believe it, because I've never seen anybody I know on television. There's Laurie holding a microphone and walking in the yard of a huge prison. "This is MCI-Cedar Junction," she says, "formerly known as Walpole, one of the state's maximum security prisons."

I glance over at Laurie sitting next to me on the sofa. Then I look back at the TV. She has so much make-up piled on that she looks like one of those store mannequins whose face never changes.

"Today I'm visiting one of Massachusetts's most notorious criminals . . ."

Dad? I swear, the guy she's standing next to looks like Dad!

"Andy, move back from the screen," Jeff says.

When I look up close I can see it isn't really my dad, but it sure could have been. Mom took me to visit him in a prison that looked like this. It was scary because they made us take off our shoes and socks and empty our pockets before we could go in. That was to make sure we weren't hiding anything like a knife to give him. I thought we were going to have to walk around barefoot the whole time, but they gave us back our shoes when we got to the other side of a huge steel door. Mom held my hand the whole time, even though I was nine years old.

I was surprised when we got inside the yard because the prisoners didn't have uniforms on like you see in movies. They were all wearing dark pants and white shirts, like salesmen in a store. We sat at a picnic table and talked. Dad gave us each a kiss, but he wasn't allowed to pick me up and twirl me around like he always did at home. He had to keep his hands on top of the table where the guards could see them. It was odd seeing Dad following all of their rules. At home he made the rules.

"Well," Jeff says, "what did you think of Laurie?"

Suddenly on the screen there's a guy dumping Pepsi on some kid's head—it's a commercial. Laurie and the prison are gone, and I can't remember a thing about her story except that the prisoner looked like Dad. "It was cool."

"Thank you," Laurie says. "It's the first time that man has talked to a reporter. I'm proud that he trusted me to do a good job telling his story."

Jeff puts his arm around her and gives her a kiss. "Laurie is very good at her job—the best reporter in Boston," he says. "You should be proud of her."

Yeah, I guess I should be, but it feels awful strange having a mother to be proud of.

Mashed potatoes, biscuits, corn on the cob—all right! Dinner looks good so far. But then she has to ruin it by bringing out this big plate of steak. I'm going to gag right here. How can anybody eat cow?

"What's the matter?" Jeff asks me. He's pretty good at knowing when I don't like something.

"I'm a vegetarian."

"You don't eat meat?" Laurie says.

Boy is she dumb. "That's what vegetarian means."

"The Home never mentioned that," she says. "And you ate hamburgers when we took you to Friendly's and Six Flags and the bowling alley."

"I just became a vegetarian, like last week, 'cause I saw this magazine with pictures in it of cows getting slit open and hung up on hooks. It was pretty gross."

She reaches across the table and stabs my piece of steak, then drops it on Jeff's plate. She looks kind of angry, but what do I care? A kid shouldn't have to eat cow if he doesn't want to.

So I load up on mashed potatoes and biscuits, and I'm feeling pretty good. After a dinner like that I don't mind clearing my plate to the kitchen, like they made us do at The Home. "Thank you," she says as I hand it to her, like it's some big deal. What does she think, that I don't know any manners?

Now for some TV time. Oh crap, he's sitting in the living room and spreading out all of his papers. He might not like me turning on the TV. I better pretend to be interested in what he's doing first. "What's up?"

"I'm sorting some papers from my last few years," he says.

"What kind of papers?"

"These are my lecture notes. I'm a high school English teacher, remember? But I'm taking the year off."

"Cool." Okay, enough about him. I'll just grab the clicker and see what's on. Soccer—no. Home shopping, news—no, no. One of those women's channels where everyone's always crying—no. The religion channel, heck no . . . all right! MTV videos. Now we're cruising. And it's one I've never seen. There are five cheerleaders rapping some song and shaking their pompoms and everything else.

"That's enough of that."

Oh man, I hate that kind of voice bossing me around. "What? I can't watch TV?"

"Not that sort." Before I know it Jeff takes the remote from me and changes channels. No more cheerleaders.

"You mean, 'cause it's IN-a-PRO-priate?" That's what adults always say when they don't want you to watch something cool. He clicks past a football game and more news and something in Spanish and then lands on Nickelodeon. Wow—they're starting an all-night Donna Reed Festival! José and I used to watch her reruns every afternoon at The Home. "This is great. Donna Reed kicks butt. You're going to watch too, right?"

"You've seen Donna Reed before?"

What, is he kidding? "Sure, haven't you?"

"Yeah, as a kid. But I didn't know . . ."

"Quiet, okay, here's the song . . ." On the TV, Donna's helping everyone get out the door in the morning. "Watch right there. She's going to give the kid his lunch, and then

the father is going to come back for . . . you know, a kiss."
The actors do as I say, just as always.

After four episodes of Donna Reed, including my favorite—
where Donna goes on strike because nobody appreciates
her—I'm ready for bed. There's only one problem—I need
something to read. Ever since Mom started leaving me alone
at night, I have to read before going to sleep. You might say
it's a habit. "You have any good books in this house?" I ask
Laurie. Okay, it's a stupid question. The shelf over the fire-
place is filled with paperbacks and the bookcase on the wall
is so jammed that the glass doors won't even close.

"No," she says, "we only buy bad books."

"What I mean is, do you have any books that wouldn't
bore a kid to death?"

"How about this one?" she says, holding up what she's
reading, *Seven Years in Tibet*. "It's about an Austrian soldier
who escapes into the highest mountains on earth during
World War II and meets people who have never seen a white
man before."

"That sounds okay, but books are better when they're
about stuff that never really happened. You got any about
magic?"

She gets up from the sofa and goes to the bookshelf.
She pulls out a couple of dusty old books that look about a
hundred years old. One of them is called *Gulliver's Travels*.
That sounds interesting. "What's it about?"

"A man named Gulliver takes a voyage and finds himself in some strange lands, like Lilliput, where the people

are no bigger than your fingers." She opens up to the picture on the first page, and there are dozens of little people nailing down Gulliver with string.

"Okay, you can read this to me."

"I thought the book was for you?" she says, but I know she really wants to read it to me. Adults always want to read to their kids. José told me that.

I just have to make up some reason. "My eyes hurt, you know, because of getting pond scum in them today from Walden, so I need you to read to me."

She says yes, of course, but she makes me brush my teeth first. Then it's a quick leap onto my bed to hear about Gulliver. "I'm ready. Read."

"This bed isn't made for jumping on," she says.

"Okay, I won't do it again." At least while she's around.

She begins reading. "My father had a small estate in Nottinghamshire; I was the third of five sons. He sent me to Emanuel College in Cambridge, at fourteen years old. . . ."

It's a pretty boring start for a book, so I figure it's a good time to sort through my last trash bag of stuff. I dive into it with my hand and pull out my old slinky, which got mangled when Lubby sat on it at The Home. Next thing I find is my bag of plastic army men they gave out last Christmas. There's a rifleman and the bazooka guy and my favorite, the flamethrower. That's what I'd be in a war—flamethrower, destroyer Andy Fleck. I reach in the bag again and feel something small and furry, one of my little stuffed animals. That reminds me, where's Ted?

"Andy, are you listening?"

"I can't listen until I find Ted. I don't know where he is and I can't sleep without him."

"Who's Ted?"

Who's Ted? Is she crazy? Think, Fleck, think. You had him in the car, and then you came in the house, and later when you brought all the stuff up you had Ted under your arm. And you put him . . . under the bed! That's it, so he wouldn't get lost. I swing myself over the side and pull him out. "This is Ted."

"He looks like a giant marshmallow," she says, "with a couple of buttons on his face."

"They're not buttons. They're real . . . something. I don't know what."

"He's very handsome."

"Ted's my main bear. He kind of takes care of all the others."

"The others?"

It's time to show her the whole bag full of stuffed animals—the rabbits, snakes, dogs, and, of course, the smaller bears. She closes her book on her finger, so I figure she really is interested in my stuffed animals. I tell her a little about each one, like his name and how I got him. Except I don't mention that Dad won Ted for me. "And this isn't even half of them. The rest are at The Home. They only let me have ten out at a time because they said I didn't need any more than that. They kept the others in a closet somewhere. I don't think animals should be kept in a closet, even if they are stuffed, do you?"

"No, I think they need to breathe, just like people."

"So I can have them all out here?"

I think she's going to say yes right away but she says, "How many are there?"

"Twenty-two. You think I'm weird, right, 'cause I'm twelve and I still sleep with stuffed animals?"

"No, I don't think that's weird. I had a stuffed Easter rabbit that I took to college."

"Yeah, but you're a girl. You're supposed to do dumb things like that. Boys aren't supposed to sleep with stuffed animals when they're my age."

"Well, that's for you to decide," she says as she opens up the book again. "You can sleep with them until you're thirty and I wouldn't care. Now where was I?"

"Skip the boring stuff. I want to hear about the Littleputtans."

"That's 'Lilliputians.'"

"Whatever."

"Okay, so Gulliver goes to sea and he gets into a ship-wreck—you want to hear about that?"

"Naw, I heard about shipwrecks before."

"Well, he makes it to shore, and he falls asleep on the beach because he's so exhausted. He wakes up and . . . 'I attempted to rise, but was not able to stir; for as I happened to lie on my back, I found my arms and legs were strongly fastened on each side to the ground; and my hair, which was long and thick, tied down in the same manner. I likewise felt several slender ligatures across my body'—a ligature," she says, "that means a thread that's tying something."

Yeah, great, just keep reading. This isn't school.

"—ligatures across my body, from my armpits to my thighs. I could only look upwards, the sun began to grow hot, and the light offended my eyes. I heard a confused noise about me, but, in the posture I lay, could see nothing except the sky. In a little time I felt something alive moving on my left leg, which advancing gently forward over my breast, came almost up to my chin; when, bending my eyes downwards as much as I could, I perceived it to be a human creature not six inches high, with a bow and arrow in his hands, and a quiver in his back."

Close your eyes, Gulliver, go back to sleep and maybe those Lilliputians will disappear. It's time to sleep, sleep, sleep . . . hey, why's she closing the book? "What are you doing?"

"I'm stopping for tonight," she says. "You're falling asleep. It's been a long day for everybody."

"But I wanted to hear what happens to Gulliver."

"Then maybe I'll read to you tomorrow night."

"And every night after that?"

She tucks the sheet around my legs even though it's still summer and not cold at all. "We'll see." My eyes close again, and next thing I know she kisses me right on the forehead! "Sleep tight, and don't let the bedbugs bite." One of my other mothers used to say that to me each night, but hard as I try, I can't remember which.

Here we go again. Another family, another house, another room to go to sleep in. This makes seven—eight, if you count the woman with the shelf full of china dogs that I knocked over when I tripped going into her house. I can still see that lady running after Al's car, waving and shouting for her to come back and get me. Al said I'd set the world's record for the shortest placement in a foster home—twenty seconds.

Now I've made it through one day here and they haven't kicked me out. Maybe I'll try for my longest record, which is five months with Conner. I could have stayed with him forever if it weren't for his wife. She was a real pain.

Jeff and Laurie seem pretty okay. For one thing, they aren't weird. What I mean is, they don't smell like beer or watch Home Shopping all day or eat cold spaghetti for breakfast. Their house is cool too, because I can run down the hallway in my socks and slide on the bare floors. And they have some great trees for building a fort. Tomorrow I'll go exploring the neighborhood to find somebody to play with. I saw lots of hoops in the driveways, so there must be kids around.

This time I have a room of my own. But it could be bigger. I used to have a room twice this size after Dad got busted the first time and Mom let me move into his TV room because he wouldn't be needing it for six to nine months. I had a trunk full of toys in there and I could watch television all night if I wanted to. She didn't care.

I have to get some new posters for the walls. And the bedspread has to go—it has yellow flowers on it! I'll throw it out the window if they won't buy me a new one. Why didn't they just pick a girl, if that's what they wanted? Why didn't they just pick a baby? I would've picked a baby, if I was them.

I'm going to make a sign for my door—Andy's Room. Stay Out or Die!

NINE

OKAY, THINK, FLECK. Where are you waking up now?

If I keep my eyes closed and never open them, maybe I'll be in Lilliput, like Gulliver, somewhere far away.

I haven't heard even one car go by out front. It's as quiet as a graveyard around here, which I know 'cause I slept in one the time Mom brought that crazy boyfriend home. He was drunk and getting too close to me, so I slipped down the fire escape and spent the night outside. I didn't mind. Who's going to bother you in a graveyard?

All you hear in this town are the crows yacking at each other. I bet nobody ever gets shot in this place. They wouldn't know what to do if they saw a bullet coming at them. In the city everyone knows you hit the ground and keep your mouth shut.

Laurie better make me pancakes. I ain't staying anywhere there aren't pancakes every Sunday. I bet she doesn't even know how to make them. She probably flattens them out, like a tank ran over them, so there's nothing to bite your teeth into. Maybe I'll show her the Andy Fleck Best Pancakes for Kids recipe: three eggs, a few cups of flour, some apple slices, dump on the brown sugar, and smear cinnamon on top. I can taste them now. Wash them down with an orange-banana shake, and that's a breakfast worth getting up for.

"Andy, I'm tired of calling you. I can hear you moving around, so I know you're awake. Do I have to come pull you out of bed?"

"No, I'm naked!" That always freezes them. I could get them in big trouble if they bust in on me and I'm bare. They could be dragged off to jail for just seeing me like that. That's what José says.

"If I'm going to make you pancakes, you have to get up right away."

Now we're talking. Al must have told her how to keep me happy.

"You've got ten seconds. I'm counting. Ten, nine . . ."

I'm not rushing. She'll make me pancakes even if I don't get up till dinner. They always do whatever I want the first weekend.

"Three, two, one . . . that's it."

"I'm up, I'm up."

"Then open the door."

Okay, I'll open the door for her. I'll do anything for pancakes.

"So," Jeff says as I'm wiping syrup from my lips, "do you want to tour the neighborhood today?"

What does he mean? They drive me around and I sit in the backseat like a moron? "You mean with you guys?"

"I meant on your own. You can take my old bike, if you

want. It's hard to get lost around here. Pretty much all the roads lead to the main route, and from there you can ask which way to head to Hawthorne Road if you need to."

Lost? Is he kidding? "I don't get lost." Okay, here goes the last bite, then I'm quitting. Seven pancakes should hold me for a couple of hours.

"Watch what you're doing, Andy," she says, and when I look where she's pointing on the table, there's this small little drop of syrup that you can barely see. She runs off to the kitchen and comes back with a wet paper towel to wipe it up. Boy, she's never seen a kid make a real mess before.

I'm off on Jeff's bike, which must be at least ten years old. The tires are so thin you can't even ride over a little crumb of dirt without feeling it in your butt. They're going to have to buy me a new bike, that's for sure. Maybe for my birthday. I wonder if they know it's coming in November. But I can't wait that long. By then it will be cold and I don't ride in the cold. I need a bike right away.

Mom and Dad would be surprised to see me now. This isn't like Boston where a kid can't ride in the street without cars running him off the road or adults yelling at him. Out here there's nothing but trees and empty roads and big houses. I could spend hours riding around looking at things. I don't even care if I get anywhere.

Oh crap, it's two o'clock, and I'm still riding my bike in the parking lot of the littlest mall I've ever seen. They told me to be back at one. They're probably sitting home right now

thinking up a punishment for me. Parents are always looking for reasons to punish you. I have to figure something to
tell them.

Outside the supermarket I see a gum machine, so I
ride up to that. Chewing on a jawbreaker always makes
me think better. I put in a quarter and out pops the gum—
along with a plastic bubble with a ring inside. That gives
me an idea.

I pedal home about the fastest any kid ever did. I leave
the bike outside and run into the house and up the playroom steps. It's good if they see you hurrying. Then I burst
through the door and start talking fast. "I'm late 'cause I
didn't know how far away I was, so it took me longer to get
back than I thought. And the other reason is that I had to
get something for someone. It's like a gift, but not for you,"
I tell Jeff. "It's for a girl—I mean a lady. So, close your eyes,"
I tell Laurie. She doesn't do it at first. Maybe she thinks
I'm going to drop a dead mouse in her hand—I did that
to Weird Joan. She deserved it too. "Come on, Laurie, it's
nothing bad. Close your eyes and hold your hand out." She
finally does, and I reach into my pocket for the small plastic tube. When I crack it open, the ring drops into her hand.
"Okay, now open your eyes."

She sees the ring and I can tell she likes it. Mothers eat
this stuff up. "This looks as nice as a diamond," she says
and holds it up to the sunlight coming in the back window.

He takes her hand and whistles. "You must have saved
a long time to pay for this."

They can't really be this dumb. Don't they know it's just

cheap purple glass? "You guys are kidding, right? I just got this out of the bubble gum machine at the market."

"Well," she says, as she slips it onto her little finger, the only one small enough, "I like it as much as a diamond."

"It's really a friendship ring, but we can't be friends, because you're supposed to be my . . . you know."

"Your mother? Mothers can't be friends?" She's asking like she really doesn't know.

"I don't think so. At least I ain't never seen it happen before."

"Not 'ain't,'" she says. "You meant to say that you 'haven't ever seen it before.'"

That's exactly what I mean—how can you be friends with somebody who's always correcting you?

It's Sunday night, and they want to go out for pizza and a movie. But I'll look dorky hanging out with parents, like I don't have any friends. And what if we go somewhere in the city and see Mom? Her boyfriends take her to the movies a lot. What could I say to her?

"So what do you think, Andy?"

Time to do the old sad-kid routine. "I guess we could go. I mean, if you really want to."

"You don't?"

Then this great idea hits me. "Why can't we just rent a movie and eat pizza here? It's raining really hard, you know, and movies are expensive, especially since I'm twelve years old now, which means adult, except I still look around eleven, so you could get me in as a little kid if you want me to lie."

"We wouldn't want you to do that," he says, like I knew he would.

"Right, so you could save lots of money if we rent a video."

"It's okay with me if we stay here," he says. "You don't care if we rent, do you?" he calls to Laurie in the kitchen.

"Why would I mind?" she says in a way that makes me think she really does.

Anyway, he takes me to the video store while she orders the pizza. He keeps pulling out all of these dopey war movies and old comedies with people I never heard of. Every time I find a cool movie he flips it over and sees the R rating. He must think I've been living on Mars all my life. I bet I know more swears than he does. And sex stuff, well, maybe I haven't done anything yet, but I know just about everything that I could do.

I don't believe it. He just picked up a video called *Animal Farm*. That sounds like a baby movie to me.

"*Animal Farm* is a great book," he says, "and this is the animated version, like a cartoon."

I wish they'd stop explaining everything to me. I know what "animated" means. All right, I'll be a good kid and give in. I'll watch his movie. Otherwise we'll be stuck in this video store forever.

At home, Laurie makes us eat the pizza in the dining room so I won't spill it on the sofa. As soon as we get done I put the tape in the VCR, and she keeps trying to tell me what buttons to push to make it work. I'm a kid, right? I know how a VCR works. It takes a few seconds, but then the video comes on and it's show time. Now all I need is my favorite blanket over me because of how cool it feels after the rain. It's the ratty old one I used to have on my bed at home, and I'm never giving it up. Jeff comes in with popcorn, and he gives me my own bowl while they share the other one.

I can tell right off I'm going to cry. The voice in the movie is saying how bad all the horses, pigs, and other animals have it on the farm. The owner, Mr. Jones, is drunk all the time, and he beats them. I hate that. I want the animals to beat him. Maybe they will in the end. I have to know what's going to happen. "You read the book, right, Jeff? Are the animals going to punch out the humans later?"

"If I tell you," he says, "that would spoil the story."

"Okay, but I'm warning you, if Boxer or Snowball gets killed, I'm going to be crying all over the place. I've seen *Old Yeller* about ten times and I still cry when they shoot him."

"I cry at movies all the time," Laurie says, but I don't see what that has to do with me. She's a lady and I'm a kid.

In this movie, the animals and men get into a cool fight. Boxer, the horse, runs at the men, and the birds peck at their heads. So the animals take over, and everything's pretty okay for a while. But then the pigs start running things. The bad pig, Napoleon, makes everyone obey him. He gets his hounds to chase Snowball, the good pig, from the farm, and it's time to cover my eyes. I can't watch that kind of stuff. "Did they catch him yet? Are they eating him?"

"They've disappeared into the woods," Laurie says, "so maybe Snowball gets away."

She doesn't know anything. "Pigs can't outrun dogs, even in cartoons."

This popcorn is pretty good. I have my routine down—my hand goes in the bowl, comes out with one piece, my fingers drop it in my mouth, then my hand dives back into the bowl for the next piece. I figure I'm eating one piece a second, sixty pieces a minute!

The video isn't bad. Napoleon makes up new rules for the farm. At the top of his list is this one: Four Legs Yes, Two Legs No. I love that. Animals rule. "Four Legs Yes, Two Legs No. Four Legs Yes, Two Legs No. Four Legs Yes, Two Legs No."

"Andy, that's enough."

What's she bugging me for? "Four Legs Yes, Two Legs No."

"We're trying to hear, Andy."

"Four Legs Yes, Two Legs No."

"Say that phrase one more time, and we're turning off the movie."

I'm just having fun. Why does she have to bug me? Jeff doesn't seem to care. "Say what?"

"Shut up!" she yells, and there it is—I've gotten to another mother, and it didn't even take two days. How's she going to last forever with me if she can't stand a little noise?

It's time to teach her a lesson. "You shouldn't say 'Shut up.' You should say 'Be quiet.'"

She gets up off the sofa as if she's going to do something.

Like what? Turn off the video? Send me to my room? So what? I've got enough games in there to last a week. Uh-oh, she's coming at me. Time to go into action. "Wait, I'll shut up, just look."

There's old Boxer, all broken down from working too hard. That's why I'm never going to work hard—look what happens to you. They drag him back to his stall, and he figures he's going to just lie around for the rest of his life. But then this truck pulls up to the barn, and the men drag Boxer out and throw him in the back. The old mule, Benjamin, sees something bad is happening, and he runs off to tell the other animals. But when they get back, the truck is pulling away. They grunt and moo to get Boxer's attention, and when he finally looks out of the back, he sees GLUE FACTORY printed on the truck. He kicks and stomps, but the walls of the truck hold him.

Boxer didn't do anything wrong. He's just an old horse. They shouldn't send good old horses to the glue factory. If you ask me, they should send rotten old people to the glue factory and let the horses alone. That's what would happen in my world, if I was king.

TEN

"ANDY, I NEED you to come inside!"

Laurie's calling me again . . . Andy get me this. Andy
clean up that. Andy Andy Andy. No way I'm doing another
chore today. It's still my summer vacation and I'm not
working!

"Andy?"

"I'm doing something!" She won't make me help her
now 'cause Jeff just went out and she's kind of afraid of me,
I can tell. She probably knows I blew up at Weird Joan's
and broke the windows in my bedroom. And I got so mad
at Mrs. Morrissey one time that I locked her in the basement when she was doing the laundry. It's good to have
a mother scared of you.

I came outside to look for Tiger, and I'm checking all of
her favorite spots—under the deck where she chases chip-
munks, in the lilies where she hunts for snakes, and under
the trees where she watches the birds. When I lift the
branches of the big hemlock in the center of the yard, there
she is, staring at me with her big green eyes. She looks kind
of spooky, like a devil cat.

"Okay, Tiger, time to come in."

She doesn't move, and she's too far under the tree for me to grab. But I brought my secret Tiger-catching weapon: Fancy Feast. She can't resist tuna. I pop open the lid of the can and she jumps from her hiding place and rubs against my leg.

"Not yet, Tiger, you have to beat me to the house." I take off running, and even though I have a big lead she catches me in a couple of bounds and passes me at the steps. But then she has to wait for me, because how's she going to get inside? She meows and stretches up toward the doorknob like she's going to turn it. "Paws aren't any good for opening doors, Tiger. You need fingers."

I let her in and she beats me to the kitchen, as always. When I turn the corner there's a woman standing with Laurie. I hate people showing up all of a sudden like this, because it usually means trouble. I've been moved twice from foster homes just by strange social workers showing up and taking me away.

"Andy, I want you to meet a friend of mine—Mrs. Freed."

"Just call me Joanne," the woman says. "Mrs. Freed makes me sound so old."

She has her hand sticking out at me, so I take it and give a little shake. What am I supposed to do now? I don't know how to talk to strange women.

Tiger to the rescue! She scratches up my leg, so I pick up her bowl and spoon out the Fancy Feast. Then I lay down on the tile to watch her eat.

"What do you see?"

It's the woman, Mrs. . . . . Joanne.

"When cats eat they curl their tongue around the food and flip it in their mouth. I used to watch Orange eat all the time—he was my cat before, with my other parents."

"Mind if I look too?"

She drops down on the floor next to me. I've never seen a lady do that before. It's pretty funny seeing her big face on the other side of the bowl. I start laughing and she does too, louder than I ever heard a woman. That scares Tiger. She jumps over me and runs down the hallway. When I look up, there's Laurie standing over us.

We both get up, and then Joanne takes a package from the table. "For you," she says.

This is really weird. I don't even know her. "Why are you giving me something? It's not my birthday."

"It's a welcome present. I'm welcoming you to Laurie and Jeff's family."

That's a good enough reason for me. I tear at the ribbon, but it's tied so tight I have to bite through it. Then I rip off the paper and open the box. Inside is a beautiful blue yo-yo, like the one José had at The Home. I'm pretty bad at yo-yoing, to tell you the truth.

"It's a yo-yo," Laurie says.

"Yeah, I know that."

"No good?" Joanne says. "I can take it back for something else."

"No, I don't want anything else. I'm going to learn to do tricks, like around-the-world and rock-the-cradle and some others I'll make up myself." I spin the yo-yo down and jerk it up like José showed me, but it comes back only halfway and then falls again.

"What do you say?"

Why does Laurie have to butt in like that? I was going to say thank you. I just forgot for a moment. "Thanks. Nobody ever gave me a present just for coming to a house before."

"Well, you deserve it," Joanne says. "I'm very happy you're here."

I know I'm supposed to say I'm happy too, but I just can't get my mouth to do it.

I've been playing in the yard with my yo-yo for an hour at least. I've made up three new tricks—rocket blastoff, crawling spider, and pouncing cat, which I also call Tiger's pounce. The yo-yo almost never dies on me now. I'm not as good as José yet, but I'm getting close.

It's hotter than anything outside, so I head in the back door to get out of the sun. I try the living room and my bedroom, but they're hot too, even with a couple of fans on. Why don't these people have air conditioning? I need some place dark and cool where Laurie can't find me, and as I walk down the hallway I think of just the spot—the towel closet. I've seen Tiger go in there, and I figure that if she likes it with all of her fur, it must be cool. I take out all of the sheets and towels and stack them on the next shelf up so Laurie won't yell at me. Then I crawl in, curl up, and pull the door shut—except not all the way. I don't want to be trapped in here forever.

There's not much to do in a closet except sleep and

think. I'm not sleepy, so I start thinking about how fast
Al moved me this time. I only went on visits with Jeff and
Laurie six times. A month ago I hadn't even met them.
And now here I am living in their house. I asked Al what
the hurry was and she said it was The Plan to move me in
before school started. She's always got some plan for me
that's supposed to be perfect. But if her plans are always so
great, how come I've been bounced around so many times?
Al would just say things haven't worked out, and now I
have the best chance ever for a home, so I better not blow
it. I know her answers by heart. I don't even have to ask the
questions anymore.

"Andy? Are you in your room?"

It's Laurie again. Every five minutes she comes looking
for me to do some little thing, like take the trash out or get
something from the garage. She's got legs, so how come
she doesn't do this stuff herself, like before I came here?

"Andy, I want you to say hello to someone."

God, another visitor. Is everybody coming to see the new
kid today?

"Andy?"

She's right outside the closet now.

"Where are you?"

"Here!" I push out the door and she jumps back like I'm
some wild animal.

"Andy," she says, "you scared me to death."

"No, I didn't. You're not dead."

"What are you doing in there?"

"Thinking."

She doesn't know what to say to that because how can you yell at a kid for thinking? She holds out the phone in her hands. "It's my mother. She wants to say hello to you."

"You've got a mother? She must be really old."

Laurie covers the mouthpiece. "She's only seventy-five."

I whistle at that because seventy-five sounds old to me. I never talked to anybody that age before. I can't imagine even being twenty-five. I take the phone and listen, but nobody says anything.

"Say hello," Laurie says.

"Hello."

"Is this Andrew?" the lady says.

"Yeah. Andy."

"Well, Andy, I hear you're going to be my grandson."

"I guess so."

"I'm very pleased to know that. And I want to meet you as soon as possible."

"Okay."

"I live in Florida, and I was thinking the whole family might come down for Thanksgiving."

"Sure."

"We might even drive over to Disneyworld, if you're interested in that sort of thing."

Disneyworld—is she crazy? Sure I'm interested. "You live near there?"

"Yes, it's about a half hour away."

"So you must go there all the time, right?"

"Whenever I have someone to go with. I'd love to take you."

"Sure, that would be great."

"Don't tell Laurie, though—she's not a big fan of amusement parks. We'll sneak off together."

"Okay, I won't tell."

"See you at Thanksgiving then. Good-bye."

"Bye."

"What won't you tell?" Laurie asks when I give her back the phone.

"It's a secret between Grandma and me—you wouldn't want me to break a promise, would you?"

Imagine that—I've got a grandmother who loves Disneyworld.

Laurie said the closet isn't the place for a boy to spend a Saturday afternoon, so I decided to explore the playroom. Jeff told me I could look at anything I want to down here as long as I'm careful. The first thing I find is an old toy chest that must have been his when he was a kid. There are cool metal soldiers and tanks in it, and I'll play war with them as soon as I make a friend. There are a million Legos too. I'm going to build a whole city when I have time.

I can see more interesting stuff on top of a large bookshelf, so I pull up a chair to reach it. First thing I take down is a long narrow case. I figure it's some kind of music instrument, but when I open it up there's two shiny pieces of wood, thick as broom handles. I take them out and screw them together—it's a pool cue! I'm ready to get down when I see a small box. Inside there's a baseball with a name written on it. Just then I hear the floor squeak upstairs, meaning someone is coming. That's a good warning signal for when I'm doing something down here I shouldn't be. I hop off the chair just as Jeff comes down the steps.

"Hey, what're you up to?"

"Nothing."

"What do you have there?"

"A baseball. I found it on top of that shelf. I'm not hurting it."

"I can see that. You know it's valuable because it's autographed, right?"

Valuable, huh. That's interesting. "Like how valuable?"

"I don't know for sure. But it's signed by Joe DiMaggio. You ever heard of him?"

Yes, no, maybe—I don't know. You might as well pretend, Fleck. Remember, he loves baseball. "Yeah, I think so."

"He played for the New York Yankees with Babe Ruth. And he had the longest hitting streak ever—fifty-six games, I think it was. He was married to Marilyn Monroe. You know who she was?"

"Sure, my dad showed me her poster once. She's the one with her dress blowing up in the picture."

"That's her."

"So how did you get the ball?"

"Laurie did a story on baseball and interviewed DiMaggio. She took a baseball along and asked him for his autograph."

This seems strange to me—the wife traveling all around working and making money, and the guy sitting home doing nothing. I've lived in strange families before, but not like this. "Can I ask you something?"

"Sure."

"You won't yell at me or nothing?"

"Depends whether your question is worth yelling about."

"You don't work, right?"

"I'm taking a year off, remember? It's called a sabbatical—teachers do that sometimes and then go back to their job."

"So you get to just lie around the house and let her make money for you?"

He laughs at my question, so I guess it doesn't bug him. "I'm not exactly lying around the house. I'm working on some new teaching modules for my English class, and I'll be looking after the house and you. That's one reason I took the time off."

"You're like a housewife now?"

"Well, sort of, I guess. Except I'm not a wife, and I'd look pretty stupid in a dress, don't you think?"

"I've seen guys in dresses before. They got them in Boston."

He must not want to talk about that because he changes the subject fast. "By the way, school starts in three days."

School—why does he have to bring that up? "I know. You don't have to tell me everything."

"I was thinking that tomorrow afternoon we could go to a ball game."

"What kind of game?"

"The Red Sox, at Fenway Park. You ever been there?"

"Sure, about forty times."

"Really?" he says. "Who's your favorite player?"

What's he asking that for? Doesn't he believe me? Do I have to name every player on the team for him? "Sometimes I like them all, if they're winning, and then I hate them all if they're losing."

"Okay, well, do you want to go with me?"

This sounds interesting, just us guys going out, no mother allowed. "Only us, right? I mean, nobody else?"

"Laurie has to work so I only bought two tickets."

"Okay then, I'll go."

So he takes me to Fenway Park, and it's this smelly brick place about a hundred years old. I've seen it from the outside before, but never inside. The seats are sticky with gum and candy, and there's this boring scoreboard about a mile away. Jeff says people come to see Fenway as much as the game. Boy, people are really stupid.

He buys me a program and tells me to hang over the rail near the dugout before the game and call out to the players for autographs. So I do that with about a dozen other kids, but the players just keep running onto the field and throwing balls to each other like they don't hear us. But I can tell they do.

After the game starts he buys me Crackerjacks and a soda. After the first inning he gets me a hotdog, and then some ice cream and peanuts. He hasn't said no to anything I've asked for!

"Your first time here, isn't it?"

I'm trying to watch the game and lick the top scoop of my ice cream before it falls off, so I forget that I told him before that I'd been here lots of times. It's not easy keeping straight what I wanted to do and what I actually did. "I would have gone to lots of games if my dad didn't have to be away so often. I think he was a salesman or something. He'd sort of drop in for a couple days and then he'd have to go away again."

"That must have been hard on you."

The Red Sox pitcher throws a strike, and the crowd cheers like it's a big deal. So I cheer too. "It wasn't really hard because, I mean, he wasn't exactly a perfect father when he was home, you know. Like he used to hit my mom sometimes for going out with other guys when he wasn't around. They used to fight a lot. The first thing I can ever remember was them throwing things at each other over my crib."

"Your crib? I don't think you can remember back that far."

Boy is he wrong. "I was still in my crib when I was five 'cause they didn't have the money to buy me a bed until then. I used to push the sides down and climb out myself— that's how old I was."

"Well then, I guess you could have remembered them throwing things over your crib."

When the seventh inning comes, Jeff gets up to stretch, and then everybody stands up and they all start singing, even the drunk guys. "Take me out to the ball game, take me out with the crowd . . ." He tries to get me to sing, but I don't sing in front of anybody, and besides, I don't know all of the words. Then he says, "I have to hit the restroom. You need to go?"

No way. Even if I did have to, I'd hold it forever rather than go in this place. He takes off in a run so as not to miss much of the game. After a few more pitches, a foul ball comes heading my way. Everybody stands up to grab for it, so I do too, but the ball sails over our heads. When I turn around, I see Jeff standing in the aisle with his hands up. The ball hits his fingers and bounces away. The guy behind him grabs it. I can't believe it—I could have had a real Red Sox baseball!

When he comes back to his seat, everybody laughs at him for dropping the ball. I'm not laughing because I really wanted a baseball and he should have caught it. My real dad would have caught it.

The game keeps going and going. Jeff says extra innings are exciting, but it just seems extra boring to me because nobody's hitting a home run. I have plenty of time to look around, and I see this giant flashing sign making crazy patterns over the outfield wall. It's got to be the Citgo sign, the same one I could see from Mom and Dad's.

"See that?"

"The old Citgo sign?"

"I could see it from my bedroom if I crawled out on the ledge."

"Sounds dangerous."

"Yeah, Mom told me not to."

"But you still did it?"

"Sure."

"That's one good thing about changing families," he says.

"You get the chance to start over. You could try listening better to what adults tell you."

Al tells me this all the time too—listen to your parents. Everybody seems to forget what kind of parents I've had. "You mean like listening to my mom when she told me I didn't have to go to school and my dad when he wanted me to steal steaks from the market? Or how about Weird Joan when she told me to pee in a bottle in the car because she didn't want to stop? Or when Dumb Donald gave me his BB gun and told me to shoot the rabbits in his yard, should I have done that?"

Jeff doesn't answer for a while. He acts like he's watching the game, but I know he heard me. "I guess you're right," he finally says. "You've been getting some bad advice from parents most of your life. But that stops right now with Laurie and me, I promise. You understand?"

"Yeah, I understand," I say, but my words are lost in the roar of the crowd. Everybody stands up. I stand up too, but I can't see what's happening over all of the adults. Sometimes I think the world would be a lot better if there were just kids in it no bigger than me.

ELEVEN

WHAT A DRAG—another first day of school. At least it's not like that pretend school at The Home where they gave us baby books to read and crayons to draw with and puzzles to do instead of math. I guess they figure you're stupid just because you don't have a family. I'm not stupid. I have an IQ of 123, which I know because they gave me a test a couple of months ago. I should have bombed it on purpose because afterward my shrink said that my IQ showed I had a lot of potential and I should be getting As when I get back to a real school.

Well, I also got ADD, which is Attention Deficit Disorder. All the doctors tell me that. I can't keep my mind on one thing for very long because something else comes along and my brain says, "Hey, that's more interesting." So I start thinking about that other thing rather than the first thing. Then a third thing comes along and a fourth and fifth, and by that time I can't remember what I'm supposed to be doing in the first place.

Like, if a parent tells me to take the trash out, I probably won't do it right away, because I'll be busy listening to my Walkman, and what kid jumps up to take out the trash anyway? After getting yelled at a few times I'll go for the trash. But on the way there I'll see something, like a tennis ball or toy car or cards. It might even be something pretty dumb, like a stapler. Before you know it I've got that stapler in my hand and I'm looking around for something to staple. When I'm done stapling a few things together, I'll probably go back to my room to listen to my tapes again. In a few minutes I'll get yelled at for not taking the trash out.

It doesn't seem fair to me that people with ADD get yelled at all the time for forgetting. I mean, how is it my fault that I forget something that I can't remember? It's like with José and his little hand halfway up his right arm. He thinks that's why his mother gave him up—because of his deformed arm. Well, José is a really fast runner and he's wicked smart and he can add all kinds of numbers in his head. But he's terrible at basketball because he only has the one good hand. Nobody yells at him that he isn't trying or he should play better. But they always yell at me to do better even though I was born with this problem called ADD. That isn't fair.

"It's 6:15, Andy. Time to get up."

I can hear both of them in the hall. They're laughing and talking like this is Christmas or something. What are they so happy about?

"Come on, Andy, you don't want to be late on your first day."

I don't want to go at all. I'm tired of going to new schools where I don't know a single kid. They're probably all preppies or jocks. They'll hate me because I don't dress like them and act like them. I'll probably be the only kid in baggy jeans. I know somebody's going to knock into me and I'm going to have to give them the old elbow to the ribs, like Dad showed me. He says that the guy who gets in the first punch usually wins, so you're stupid if you don't hit first and ask questions later.

"Andy?"

"What?"

The door opens and Jeff's standing there in his bathrobe. Sure, he wants *me* to get up and go to school but he can go back to sleep since he doesn't have a job. He's tapping me on the legs and pulling off my cover. I hate that.

"Okay, okay, I'm coming."

He leaves my room and I get up and pull my favorite clothes from the drawer. You have to look good the first day, so I'll wear my baggiest jeans and my T-shirt from an arcade in Boston called Bonkers. It says BONKERS on the front, and on the back there's a picture of a kid pounding his head against the wall. Lots of people think he looks like me. If there are any skater kids in this school, they'll know I'm one of them.

I drag myself to the kitchen and Laurie says, "We bought Grape Nuts and Cheerios for you, or you can have Super Natural Granola if you like that better."

My mouth is too tired to say a word, so how is it going to eat?

"If you don't want cereal, we have toast and English muffins. Or I could make you some eggs."

Stop, please. I'm going to gag hearing about all this

⇒94⇐

food. She really expects me to eat now? It's not even six-thirty. I have to set her straight. "I never eat breakfast before school."

"No? Then what happens around ten o'clock when you don't have enough energy to stay awake in class?"

That's easy. "I fall asleep." Okay, feet, take me to the bathroom. I might as well brush my teeth before they yell at me about that. When I come back down the hallway with my schoolbag, she's standing there with a glass of orange juice and a banana in her hands.

"How about just this?"

"I already brushed my teeth. I can't eat anything now."

"You can take the banana with you." She practically shoves it into my pocket. Then she opens the front door for me.

"Wait a second," he calls from my room. "Your bed still needs to be made—remember, we talked about the morning routine."

"You don't want me to miss my bus on the first day, do you?"

"You've got time. Laurie's watching for it."

This must be how they treat you in jail, telling you what to do every second. But I'm too tired to fight. So I drop my bag at the door and head back to my bedroom. Jeff stands there watching me make my bed like I'm a four year old. "There, can I go now?"

"Sure."

"Don't miss the stop on the way back," she says as I come back down the hallway. "It's the number seven bus.

You get off right after it turns on Hawthorne. Do you want me to write that down?" She grabs a pen and paper off the table and actually starts writing it!

I have to get to the door fast, before they try to pin a name tag on my shirt. "I wasn't born yesterday, you know. I can get to school and back."

"Your pills!" she yells, like I'll drop dead on the bus if I don't take them. She runs to the kitchen and back with a glass of water and my Ritalin.

"Now can I go?"

"Sure," Jeff says. "Have fun."

Fun at school? Yeah, right. "Smell ya later."

You've seen one prison, you've seen them all. That's what my father used to say. Schools are like prisons and you just have to do your time.

I've gone to tougher schools than this. The kids look like they've got money to burn. God, all these nerds lugging piles of books down the halls. The next one that bumps into me I'm going to send into orbit. If they think they can push me around just because I'm new they'll find out different fast. I've been new before.

I don't know where I'm going, and I don't care. This place doesn't make sense. The homeroom teacher with the brown mole on her neck told me to go through the library and take a left and then a right, so here I am staring into a cinder block wall. Maybe she said take a right and then a left. Who knows?

There's the late bell. Oh well. So I miss first period—it's

just baby math anyway. Who needs that again? I can multiply fractions and figure percentages. What's the use of going to class if they're just going to teach you something you already know?

"Need help, son?"

No, I'm just staring at the wall 'cause I'm a moron. Who is this guy wearing a fat tie with cows on it? He probably thinks he's really cool. And what's this "son" stuff? I'm nobody's son at the moment.

"What class are you supposed to be in?"

All right, Fleck, chill out. Don't scare the teachers on the first day. "Math, sir." Adults eat it up when you talk to them politely. "Could you please tell me where Mrs. Gagnon's class is?"

The guy takes my arm like I'm mental and turns me back the way I came. Steady, Fleck, just move away from him slowly. Don't make a scene.

"Walk about ten steps down and take a right at the first hallway." He points his hand, like I don't know which way right is. "Mrs. Gagnon's room is the second door on the left."

Right and then left, and here I am at math. Great, the kids are already sitting down. Now I have to walk in like some geek who can't even find his way to class. Take a deep breath, Fleck. Make yourself look bigger than you really are. That's the way cats do it when a dog spots them. Don't let them think you're scared.

"Andrew Fleck, I presume," the teacher says.

"You presume right."

A few kids laugh, like I've said something hysterical.

"I understand you're new here, Andrew. Welcome to our school. You may sit in any vacant seat."

Andy, the name is Andy. There are only three open desks. I pass by the first one and the second one because they're right under the teacher's eye, and then I see a third desk next to a girl who looks interesting. She's got a streak of purple down the back of her hair and a skull inked on her forearm. Maybe this school won't be so bad after all. She's looking down at her book like she doesn't see me coming, but I know she does. If I wanted a girlfriend right now, she's the one I'd go for.

It's 3 p.m., drop off time at home. I can see Jeff watching from the window of his office as I get off the bus. Why doesn't he just meet me at the curb like I'm some first grader? By the time I get to the door, he's there opening it for me. "Hey, kiddo, how did it go?"

"Okay." I take my schoolbag to the room and toss it on my bed. Then it's back to the kitchen. "I'm starving. That lunch she gave me wasn't big enough to fill a flea." In the refrigerator I find a root beer and grapes, and in the pantry there's a whole jar of roasted peanuts. That will hold me for a while. Now it's time to find Tiger.

I head out the back door. It takes a couple of minutes of calling her before she shows herself. It's like magic—I turn around and suddenly she's sitting in the middle of the yard watching me. She doesn't run anymore when I go to pick her up because she knows me now. "Come on, Tiger, I'm going to take you in the house for a treat. Every day when I come home from school you get one."

Tiger is the best cat I've ever had, and I'm going to treat her right. "When I get rich," I whisper in her ear, "I'm going to buy you a gold collar so you can live like a rich cat." She rubs her face against mine, so I know she understands.

"It's just us for dinner," Jeff says as he puts a plate of tuna salad on the dining-room table, along with sliced tomatoes and cucumbers, baked beans, rolls, and applesauce. "Laurie's working late."

"Great," I start to say but stop before the word gets all the way out of my mouth. As we sit at the table he opens a folder of newspaper clippings. "What's that?"

"These are some articles I cut from the paper the last few days, things you might be interested in hearing about."

This sounds like school again. How come they're always trying to make me learn stuff? It's just my luck that I'm living with a teacher. "I always just talk at dinner. I never had to listen to crap from the newspaper before."

"Don't talk like that."

"You mean I can't even say 'crap'? What is this, church or something?"

"No, but you don't need to talk like that. Just listen while I read. You might actually find these interesting." So he reads me this lame story about some Indian guy from India who started bicycling around the world. He left his home with no money in his pocket and only one change of clothes. After eleven years he's gone 198,000 miles.

That seems strange to me. "How come this guy has biked 198,000 miles, and he hasn't gone around the world yet?"

Jeff looks back at the story, but he can't find an answer. I got him on this one. "I guess he wasn't taking a very direct route."

"The whole earth is only like 22,000 miles around, right, if you go in a straight line?"

"Something like that," he says. "At the equator."

"Then that guy must be crazy, or lost."

Jeff nods that I'm right. One point for Fleck. I dive into the beans and rolls and let him babble on. He doesn't know how to make beans—where's the ketchup? I like to soak up the bean juice with my roll. That's how Dad does it.

"The next story is about the human body," Jeff says. "According to this professor, if you never cut your hair it would grow to—well what would you guess?"

"Twenty feet."

"No, four feet, and then it would stop."

That doesn't seem like much to me, but I guess I have to believe it since it's in the newspaper. Anyway, I'm getting full and need a break from eating. So I push my chair away from the table and rock back on the legs.

"You need to eat your vegetables, Andy."

"Who said I wasn't? You shouldn't be telling someone to eat more when they aren't even done yet."

"That's not the way to talk to a parent."

He's pulling the old "I'm the parent" routine already. Every adult I've ever lived with says the same thing. But how come they're so special? How come they can talk to a kid one way but we have to talk to them another way? That's what I'd like to know. Besides, he's not really my father. Maybe he will be someday, but he isn't yet.

I can't believe I have to go to bed at nine-thirty. Schools are stupid, making kids get up so early. Everybody knows the first classes each day are a waste. Nobody's awake.

"Time for lights out," Jeff calls as he walks down the hallway toward my room. I sink under the covers.

"Andy? Are you under there?" He's poking in the mound of covers like he really isn't sure. His hand jabs my stomach, then my arm, then . . . I chomp on it with my mouth.

"Okay," he says, patting my head, "time for you to hibernate for the night."

Since he's goofing around, I figure I can show him what I did. I pull the comforter off my face and turn off my light. "Look up at the ceiling."

He does, and my universe of little gold stars starts glowing.

"Where did they come from?"

I can't tell if he's mad or not, so I won't admit to anything right off. "They kind of flew out of my bag and onto the ceiling. You don't mind, do you?"

"No, they're neat."

"Okay, so I put them there. My . . . well, somebody gave them to me once, but I never had a ceiling where I wanted to put them before. At The Home they don't let you put stuff up because you could be leaving any day and the next kid might not like it."

The room is quiet and dark. It's strange having this guy I've only known for about a month hanging around my bed. Dad never did that. Even when he wasn't in jail he didn't spend much time at home. He always said he was out working.

Jeff's straightening my puppets on the bookshelf and looking at my school books. I think he's just doing these things to have a reason for staying in my room. That's okay with me. I don't want to go to sleep yet, and it's kind of cool having a father around. It gives me a chance to ask him some stuff I've been thinking about, like, "Do you think we're going to blow ourselves up or burn up—I mean, like how we're going to end the world?"

He sits down at the bottom of my bed and leans back. "I'd say we're just going to ruin the earth slowly over thousands of years until there's nothing much good left to it."

"Not me. I think we're going to blow ourselves up."

"I used to worry about that when I was little," he says, "because it seemed like we might get into a nuclear war with the Russians. We even had air-raid drills in school where we'd crouch in the hallways and cover our heads."

"You were covering your head against a nuclear bomb dropping on you?"

"Sounds pretty stupid, doesn't it? Anyway, kids today aren't supposed to worry about the world blowing up."

"Who said I was worried? You ever sky dived?"

"I don't like heights, so I'm not going to be jumping out of a plane, that's for sure."

"My dad sky dives, I mean, my first dad." Jeff doesn't say

anything. Either he doesn't believe me or he doesn't want to hear about Dad again. Whatever. "I bet I could be the world's best sky diver. I'd go up in a rocket and jump out, and then I could see the whole earth and land in Disneyworld or Africa if I wanted to." Thinking about skydiving reminds me of something else I always wanted to ask Dad about. "Where's heaven? We shoot rockets into space and nobody ever sees it, so how can it be up there?"

"The universe is very, very big, Andy, much bigger than we can see, so heaven could be out there somewhere and we wouldn't know it. But heaven really isn't a physical place anyway, it's more an idea of where God lives and our souls go when we're dead. You can't see our souls when we're alive, so they wouldn't need a physical place to go to when we're dead, right?"

"I guess. You ever know anybody who was dead?"

"You mean have I known anybody who died? Sure, a few people."

"Like who?"

"I had an uncle drown when I was very young. I saw him when they pulled him from the water."

That sounds gross, a body all filled up with water. I don't want to hear about it. "Is he the only one?"

Jeff doesn't answer for a minute. I guess he's trying to remember. I know I wouldn't forget it if I saw a dead person. Finally he says, "My parents died in a car accident when I was ten years old. I saw them in their caskets before the funeral service."

I can't believe it. Ten is younger than me, and that's when

Jeff had to look at his dead parents. I could never do that. "What happened to you—they send you to a foster home?"

"No, a great aunt took me in."

"What was so great about her?"

He laughs like I've made a joke. "I mean she was the sister of my grandmother, which makes her a great aunt, not just an aunt. She *was* great, though, to take me, so I could live in my same town. The thing is, she was pretty old and kind of sick, so I had to be quiet around her all the time. That's not easy for a boy."

I figured Jeff grew up in one of those perfect families with a father who plays football in the yard with his son and they both get covered in dirt and grass stains. The mother's in the kitchen making a cake, and she always remembers where you've left your favorite cap when you can't find it before school. She reminds you to take your gym clothes too. For some reason it makes me feel better knowing that Jeff didn't have his parents for very long either.

"I'm glad you're here with us," Jeff says.

I close my eyes fast as if I'm sleeping and didn't hear him. I don't want to have to say anything back to him. I mean, I'm glad to be here too. Who wouldn't be after living at The Home? I like going to bed in this place better than any other I've been in. But every time I start liking a place I get kicked out for some reason. Like with Conner. We were getting along great, and I thought maybe they would adopt me until his wife got jealous because he was spending so much time with me. She said he wasn't paying attention to their own kid, this dopey little girl who cried all the time to get her way. So his wife ran off with their kid one day while Conner and I were out biking. When we came back we found a note on the door from her saying he had to choose between them or me. I thought maybe he'd choose me, but he didn't.

The same thing could happen again. Laurie doesn't like me as much as Jeff does, I can tell. She could get jealous of me just like Conner's wife did.

I can hear Jeff breathing. I can't open my eyes as long as he's sitting there, because he'll expect me to say that I'm glad to be here too, and that could ruin everything.

TWELVE

I DON'T KNOW what day it is. It doesn't matter because every day's the same anyway. Laurie yells at me in the mornings when I won't jump out of bed right away. Then she threatens to take away my ice cream or TV time at night. But that's like a million hours away. All I care about is getting a few more minutes of sleep. If I miss the bus, so what? They'll drive me. They won't let me stay home, that's for sure. They act like I'll go dumb forever just for missing one day of school.

After a while Jeff comes in and tries to pull the covers off me, but I know how to wrap myself up like a mummy so he can't do that. Then he starts tickling and talking to me in strange voices. It's pretty funny, so after a while I get up but not while he's standing there telling me to. I learned that trick from José back at The Home. He said you have to do some things in a family. You can't always get your way. But never do anything exactly when they tell you to, especially if they're standing there waiting. Always make them go away before you do it. That shows them who's boss.

When I get home every afternoon, the first thing I do is

go out back to find Tiger. That's pretty easy now because she knows I'm going to give her a treat. She comes running as soon as she hears the back door open.

After giving my cat a seafood Pounce I usually just hang around the house. Sometimes Jeff shoots hoops with me or throws the football around. But today I wanted to do something different. So I decided to play baseball— a least, that's what I told Jeff when I biked off an hour ago carrying this old bat of his. He told me to be careful because it was a "Ted Williams"—that's a famous guy who played for the Red Sox years ago. The bat isn't autographed. It just has his name stamped on it. They probably made tons of them.

Anyway, I rode off with the old Ted Williams in my hand for a game of mailbox baseball. We used to do this all the time at my last foster home. What you do is ride down the street as fast as you can and swing at a mailbox. It's a single every time you hit a box and a home run if you knock the whole thing off. That isn't easy because some of the boxes are really screwed down tight. If you hit a big wooden post instead of the box, the shock can knock you off your bike, which I know 'cause it happened to me a couple of times. It didn't happen today, though.

So now I'm coasting down the big hill home, and I'm feeling great because I got two singles and one home run in six swings, which is terrific batting. I wish José had been there to see it. The only problem is that the Ted Williams got a few knicks in it, and the handle cracked when it hit a

metal box. I don't see how that's my fault, though. I mean, bats are supposed to hit baseballs thrown a hundred miles per hour. They shouldn't crack just hitting a mailbox.

When I turn in the driveway I see the garage door's open, and Jeff's standing there like he's waiting for me. He'll probably go crazy seeing the busted bat, but it's too late to throw it away and say I lost it. Sometimes I wonder why I do stuff that gets me in trouble so much. The problem is, I usually wonder this *after* getting in trouble, which doesn't help much.

The only thing I can do now is deny everything, like Dad taught me. He said, "If they don't catch you red-handed, they can't prove anything." He was talking about the cops, but I think he meant parents too.

So I'll play it cool, say "Hey" to Jeff as I hop off my bike, maybe even whistle a little. Then I'll lean the bike on the wall of the garage, exactly where he told me to put it, and head upstairs.

"Hold on," he says. "I want to talk to you."

Here it comes. They always start out with "I want to talk" and then blast you.

"What were you doing out on your bike today?"

"I was riding. You just saw me come in, didn't you?"

"What were you doing while you were riding?"

"Sweating?" That's it, Fleck, make a joke. Jeff likes jokes. So how come he's not laughing?

He says, "I think you were playing mailbox baseball."

Oh man, he even knows the name for it. I could be in for big trouble. I've got to keep up the innocent act. "What's that?"

"I bet you know."

It's time to go on the offensive. "What, were you spying on me? I can't even go for a ride without being followed around?"

"I didn't have to spy on you, Andy. A woman in the neighborhood happened to see you, and she came around to tell me."

How could that be? I would have seen somebody seeing me. And even if a woman did see me, how would she know who I am or where I live? He has to be making this up. "Nobody knows me around here, so you must have followed me."

"Her son saw you too. He rides the bus with you."

I'm caught. The one kid who sees me whacking a mailbox rats on me to his mother. It must be that nerd sitting in the front of the bus.

"When you wreck a mailbox," Jeff says, "you're tampering with government property, not to mention someone's personal property."

Government property, personal property, it's all the same to me. I don't have any. It's not like I wrecked anything of Jeff's, so why is he so mad? "You going to throw me in jail for having a little fun?"

"What we're going to do is drive down the street and find the mailbox you broke. Then we'll go to the house and you can apologize and tell the person you'll pay for the damage from your allowance."

He's got to be kidding. Nobody ever apologized for all of the stuff they did to me, so why should I apologize to anybody? I try to make a run for it into the basement, but he catches my shirt and pulls me back toward the car.

"I said you're going with me."

He can't shove me around like this. He better watch out. I'll show him my fist and he'll get the idea.

"I wouldn't do that," he says.

"My dad would punch you in the face right now, if he was here."

He yanks me over to the car and practically flattens me over the front hood. "Andy, your wonderful father is in jail, where he's spent a lot of your life instead of taking care of you. So don't go pretending how great he is, because I know all about him. You can still love him, because he *was* your first father, but you don't need to act like him."

I don't like him talking about Dad like that. He wanted to be a regular father. He just couldn't help getting in trouble. I know how that feels.

"Of all people on this street," Jeff says as we walk up the gravel driveway to a small square house, "you have to pick old man Lucinski's mailbox to hit."

"What's so terrible about him?"

Jeff rings the doorbell. "You'll see."

"What do you want?" comes a yell from a window to the left of the door.

"Mr. Lucinski, I'm a neighbor of yours from down the street. Can I speak to you for a minute?"

"Speak your piece," the voice says.

Jeff moves off the front steps toward the open window where the voice is coming from. We can't see through the screen into the room, and it's like talking to a ghost. "I'm sorry to say that Andy here was playing a game in the street and knocked down your mailbox."

There's the sound of something scraping across a floor, and a dark shape comes to the window. "He yours?"

I look at Jeff and he looks at me. "Well . . . yes," he says. "I'm his father."

My father? My real father wouldn't be dragging me up the street to apologize to some crazy old man. My real father would tell him off.

"If we can't fix the mailbox ourselves, he'll pay for a new one," Jeff says. "Is that okay?"

"Doesn't seem like I have any choice, does it?" the voice asks. "The damage is done."

"Yes, I'm sorry," Jeff says and then nudges me.

"Yeah," I say toward the window, "me too."

It's only eight-thirty and he sent me to bed just because I smashed a mailbox. How was I supposed to know it was so bad to do that? We used to play mailbox baseball all the time in my last neighborhood. It's just we never got caught.

I'll show Jeff how I feel. I'm setting up my army battalion right inside the door—the riflemen and the flame throwers and the tanks and the big helicopter. As soon as he opens the door he'll get the idea. He better not cross that line or they'll blast him.

Laurie hasn't even come home yet. She's always working. I don't mind because I know I could get along with just Jeff if I tried a little harder to stay out of trouble. To tell you the truth, I did know it was wrong to knock over mailboxes. I'm not stupid. I can tell right from wrong. The problem is, doing the wrong thing is often more fun than doing the right thing. I don't know why God made things that way, but He did.

I hear the garage door go up. Sounds like an earthquake happening under my bed. When I crawl out from under my covers, I look out the window, and there's Laurie coming up the driveway in her car. A second later the whole house shakes again.

I sink back under my covers and listen for her to come up the steps from the playroom. It's almost like hearing my real mom come home late in our apartment. Except then I was alone and scared waiting for her. I'm not scared in this house with Jeff in the bedroom next door. He yelled at me about the mailbox thing and said some bad stuff about Dad, but still, he didn't hit me. I don't mind being yelled at.

I can hear her coming down the hall now. My door's open a little. She should come and check if I'm breathing, right? I mean, if I had a kid and I was out late, I'd look in on him when I came home.

The floor creaks as she comes down the hall. My door squeaks open a little, but she doesn't come in, just like I figured.

THIRTEEN

IT'S SATURDAY MORNING, and they think I'm cleaning my room like they told me to. But I shut my door and sneaked out through the window. I'm good at sneaking. A kid shouldn't be kept in on a Saturday.

It's hot and windy and perfect for climbing trees. First I tried one of the big willows, but I couldn't get up very high because the branches are so far apart. So now I'm climbing this huge pine tree next to the porch. There's lots of places to put my feet, and I bet I can get up fifty feet, higher than ever before. If only José could see me now.

I wish I had a brother to climb trees and wrestle with. Maybe they want another kid and I could tell them about José. Except he's bigger than me. I really need a little brother I can push around sometimes. I get tired of being pushed around by bigger kids.

After a while climbing gets boring, so I jump down and do a headstand under the willow where the grass is thick and soft. I count up to forty-eight before my legs start wobbling and I fall over. Then I crawl back through the grass like a soldier to the living-room window. José said that you have to learn how to spy in a new house. He said countries use spies so they can learn about their enemies, and that's why kids should too. Jeff and Laurie aren't exactly my enemies, but I still need to know stuff about them. I wouldn't have to spy if I was their real kid because I'd have already learned everything I need to know just by growing up with them.

It's weird being the only kid in the house. In my foster homes there were usually five or six of us. Jeff and Laurie showed me pictures of their families—I've got nine new cousins! But they live in other states, so I won't see them except on holidays. That sucks.

I crawl up under the living-room window where they can't see me even if they look out. I can hear Laurie talking about her TV show and how she's going to have to work late again this week and blah blah blah. Then he tells her about mailbox baseball, and she says that doesn't surprise her. What's she mean by that—she knew I'd get in trouble? What makes her so smart? She says that she peeked in on me last night when she came home and I looked so innocent. Then she says something strange, she says, "I was wondering when I was looking at Andy, what if it turns out we just don't like him?"

Not like me? What's she talking about? What if I don't like them?

Next thing she brings up the stupid DSS reports and all those people who say I'm obnoxious. So what? I already told them I was. All twelve year olds are obnoxious—at least the boys are. She says she wonders if there might be something really wrong with me, because I get angry so fast and get in so much trouble. She says that maybe they should take me to a therapist. God, I'll run away if they do that. I'm sick of going to shrinks and answering all their stupid questions. She could make up stuff to tell him so that I sound psycho. She could make up anything she wants, and who's going to believe me?

I knew Laurie didn't want me. I knew she was going to ruin it. Well, if she wants to see psycho, I can show her psycho.

I never actually made a bomb before, but I saw a kid in one of my foster homes do it. He packed it in the ground so that when it exploded, dirt shot all over the place. He got kicked out of that family the next day, which is what he was trying to do.

Now's the perfect time for me to make one right here in their backyard where they'll be sure to see it go off. I have string for a fuse and the gun powder my dad gave me that I've been hiding. All I need is Tabasco sauce. I tried sneaking in the back door to get the stuff, but Laurie saw me. She said, "Andy, I thought you were cleaning your room."

"You thought wrong," I said and kept on walking. She told me not to be smart-alecky and asked what I was doing outside.

So I told her. "Making a bomb."

"Very funny," she said, but she won't be laughing later.

I couldn't find any Tabasco sauce, so I had to ask her for it. She found a little bottle and asked why I wanted it. "I'm going to drink it," I said. She didn't believe me, so I took the cap off and I would have drunk it right there, but she stopped me. She said nobody drinks Tabasco sauce, but that's a lie. I drank it once on a dare at The Home. It wasn't so bad going down. The taste was kind of interesting, like a real, real spicy burrito. But when the Tabasco came back up from my stomach a few hours later, that tasted nasty.

Anyway, I fix the fuse into the small plastic bag of gun powder and then pour the Tabasco sauce over the bag. I think that's how this other kid did it. All that's left to do is make a big mound of dirt over everything, light the fuse, and watch the fun. Here we go. . . .

Crap. The fuse went out. Got to light it again. Now, here we really go. . . .

"Andy, are you playing with matches?" She's coming fast down the back steps. Let's go, fuse. Burn. Burn!

"Andy, what are you doing?"

"I told you before, making a bomb."

She sees the fuse and stamps it out with her big feet. Then she grabs my arm and practically drags me back to the house. I bet I could sue her for child abuse, if I wanted to.

She told Jeff, of course. She likes getting me in trouble. He went out and found the gun powder buried in the ground. He gave me the third degree—Dad said that's what it's called when the cops ask you a lot of questions. Jeff wanted to know where I got the gun powder and what I was trying to do. It's strange, because I never cared if my other dads got mad at me, as long as they didn't use their belt on my legs. But when Jeff gets mad at me, *I* start feeling bad, like I let him down.

So I made up another excuse. I told him that I was just doing a science experiment, which I was about to tell Laurie about, but she went ballistic on me and my arm still hurt from where she grabbed it. He said that maybe she had misunderstood what was going on and overreacted. I said yeah, she had overreacted, 'cause how's a kid supposed to learn anything if he doesn't try stuff?

Anyway, all day they had these talks with each other, and sometimes they got pretty loud. They practically didn't talk at all during dinner except when he read some more of those dopey newspaper stories.

So now it's bedtime and she's calling him to come out to the living room, but I have him with me in my bedroom and I'm not letting him go yet.

"Try to get to sleep right away," he says, "so you can catch up on what you missed during the school week."

"But I can't sleep unless I get read to. She said she would read to me every night, but she doesn't."

"Laurie works long hours, you know that, so she's trying to rest up a little too on the weekends."

"Then how come you don't read to me? Are you too tired from working?" I knew that would get him, since he doesn't work at all. But just then she calls to him again and he says he can't read to me tonight. Time for Plan X, which is my special trick: ask something weird—anything. "Where do blimps go at night?"

"Blimps?" he says and stops at the door. "I suppose they land in an airport, but I've never really thought about it."

Now I've got him interested. Keep up the questions. "So

they let all the gas out of the balloon every night and then it's like this big flat football lying on the ground?"

"I don't know," he says. "The pilot and passengers wouldn't want to stay up there for days, obviously, so the blimp has to land, but I don't know whether it deflates or they keep it filled with gas." He comes back into the room a step. "You know, this sounds pretty stupid, but when I was young I used to think that people rode inside the big part of the blimp and not in that little compartment underneath."

"That is pretty stupid."

"Thanks."

He turns toward the door again. Think, Fleck, think. "Do cats have accents?"

"Accents? You mean like a southern drawl?"

"Yeah, like, do they meow different in different places, like people do—talk, I mean, not meow?"

"That's an interesting question," he says as he sits down on the side of my bed.

Of course it is. José thought it up.

"I suppose different types of cats might meow a little differently, but they don't really have a developed language like we do with thousands of words. Cats just make single sounds, so there's a lot less opportunity for variation."

"Okay, now you tell me something to think about."

He thinks for a moment. "Well, when I was your age, I used to go to sleep imagining there was another world where another boy lived who happened to be named Jeffrey and looked like me and acted like me. I imagined him to be exactly the same as me, but with a world around him completely different."

"You mean like people could fly in this world or live to be a thousand years old?"

"Yeah, something like that."

"That sounds cool." Okay, Fleck, close your eyes and think up your own universe. "I'm going to imagine a world that's run by twelve year olds. They're the ones called 'adults.' Everybody older than fifteen are called 'Almost Dead,' and nobody has to listen to them, because they never make any sense and they're going to die soon anyway."

"Sounds like a world where you wouldn't need a father," Jeff says.

"You have to have a father with you, until you're eighteen, at least. That's another law I'd make—in this other world, I mean."

"Not in this world?"

"Okay, in this one too."

"That would be a good law, Andy. Now, sweet dreams."

When I open my eyes, he's gone.

FOURTEEN

I WENT EIGHT whole days without getting in trouble at school. That's a record for me. But I knew I couldn't keep it up being good. Something always happens.

My problems today started when I was getting off the bus and the girl behind me pulled the chain on my wallet. I turned around and shoved her, which is what the bus monitor saw, so I got reported. Then in art this kid kept whispering to everybody that I was adopted, like that meant I was something weird. So I accidentally on purpose knocked blue paint onto his picture, and he went crying to the teacher. In gym the coach kicked a soccer ball at me so hard he knocked me over, and everyone laughed. When he wasn't looking I threw the ball at his head, but I missed 'cause I'm not really very good at sports. He sort of figured it was me who threw it, but he didn't know for sure until this dork Ronald pointed at me. So this Nazi gym teacher got in my face and yelled at me. He said he knew I had a lot of troubles with being adopted and whatever, which is when I stopped listening. I hate it when people think they know what it's like to be adopted. They *say* they know how tough it is, but then they expect you to act like some perfect kid who's lived in a perfect family for all of his perfect life. Nobody ever taught me to be good, so how am I supposed to know how to do it?

My gym teacher kept lecturing me so long that I was sweaty and late by the time I got to science. Everybody laughed at me again when I walked into class because old Mrs. Hyde said I looked like something the cat dragged in. I got her back for that by throwing spitballs at her when she turned to the chalkboard. She told me to stand outside the room, and I told her to go jump in Walden Pond. She called the principal and he came to take me to his office, but I wouldn't move. Adults hate that when they tell you something and you just won't do it. Dad told me that teachers can get in big trouble if they touch you, so how are they going to make you do anything? Schools have stupid rules. If I were a principal, I'd just grab a kid like me and drag him down the hall.

"The straitjacket is our friend. The straitjacket is our friend. The straitjacket is our friend."

José taught me to say this whenever I want to bug some adults. It makes them think you're crazy, and then they don't know what to do with you. So that's what I kept saying every time old Principal Jones told me I better come with him to his office or else. Or else what?—call the cops on me? I don't think so.

"The straitjacket is our friend. The straitjacket is our friend."

Finally he just told all the other kids to get up and move to another classroom, leaving me sitting there alone. That didn't bother me. I had my lunch and my tape player and a book called *Frankenstein* that I took from the bookshelf at home. I could have stayed there all day.

He didn't let me, of course. About an hour later he came back in the room with Jeff right behind him. They sat in the little desks in front of me and looked pretty dopey because of how big they are. The principal went on and on about how in twenty years he hadn't ever moved a whole class. He told Jeff he had never dealt with a kid as bad as me—okay, he didn't really say this, but that's what he meant. He said that maybe I'd be better off in a school that was used to handling kids like me.

Jeff jumped out of his seat like he was going to clobber the old guy. "Another school?" he said. "We live in this town and pay taxes for this school, and this is where Andy is going to be educated. We'll deal with him at home, and you deal with him at school." That's all he said, and then we were out of there.

We're driving home now, and Jeff's not saying much. I think he's mad at having to come down to school to get me. I don't see what the big deal is. It's not like he's missing work or anything.

Anyway, I reach into my schoolbag and pull out the potato chips that this sixth grader gave me. I only asked for one little chip, but he gave me the whole bag. He probably thought I was going to hit him or something. That's the thing about having a reputation—sometimes you don't have to do anything and the kids give you what you want.

If you're kind of small, like me, and new in school, you need to get a reputation fast, or else the kids will pick on you. I guess I have one.

So I rip open the potato chip bag with my teeth and start eating, making sure to crunch really loud. If Jeff wants one, he's going to have to ask extra nice. I'm crunching and licking my fingers and he's still not talking. When I lift the bag to my mouth and pour in the crumbs, some of them spill on the seat. He still doesn't say anything. This is weird. So I roll down the window and let the bag flap in the wind. "I could let this go, if I wanted to," I say. "Then *you'd* get fined a lot of money for littering, 'cause they can't fine a kid, right?"

"Andy, what got into you today?"

So now he's talking. "What do you mean?"

"I mean all the trouble you gave the teachers. It's almost like you were doing it on purpose."

"Maybe I was."

"Why would you want to get into trouble?"

He probably never did anything wrong when he was a kid, so he doesn't know how much fun it is seeing all the teachers running around trying to deal with you. They wish they could just smack you, but they can't, so they get red in the face and all they can do is yell, yell, yell, as if that makes any difference to me. I've been yelled at all my life.

"There must be a reason," he says.

Sure there's a reason. "She told them I was adopted. Now everybody probably knows."

"What do you mean? Who said you were adopted?"

"She did—your wifey."

"Andy," he says my name like he's spitting, "don't refer to Laurie like that."

"She told the principal. She said you were going to adopt me, and now all the teachers know, and the kids too."

"The school needs to have information like that. When we registered—"

I don't want to hear his reasons. He doesn't know what it's like to have people knowing you're adopted. Besides, I'm not adopted, not yet. Al says I have to live with them for at least six months and then go to court for the adoption to be final. I've never lived with any of my foster parents that long, not even Conner. Just when I think everything's going okay something happens and the parents kick me out. So I figure, why not make trouble and get it over with right away? Why pretend they're going to keep me?

"Maybe you aren't adopting me," I tell Jeff.

"I thought that's what you wanted," he says.

"Maybe I don't want anything. Why didn't you just pick some perfect little kid, if that's what you want?"

"We don't expect you to be perfect. And you picked us, remember, at the roller-blading rink?"

"I just wanted to get out of that freaking prison they call a home." It feels good cursing out loud like that. I don't care if he cares. "I'm only living in this crummy town until I can find some place better."

"Some place better, huh?" he says like he doesn't believe me.

I'll tell him off. I'll make him mad and then we'll see

how much he wants me. "Yeah, some place where the people don't stink."

I knew that would get to him. He pulls the car off the road into a driveway. He's almost shaking. "You asked for us, now you got us," he says. "And you better watch your mouth, or you may find yourself sitting on the side of the road for a while thinking about how you talk to adults."

Yeah, right. "You can't just leave me somewhere. You have to take care of me, or else DSS will put you in jail."

"Andy, your own parents didn't take care of you," he says, "so why do you think we have to?"

That's a mean thing for him to say, that's what I think.

We didn't talk much after that. When I got home I went downstairs and turned on the new TV they bought for the playroom. It's only a thirteen-incher, but I don't care. After a while Jeff starts bugging me to come up for one of the gross dinners he makes. Where's Laurie anyway? Why can't she make the meals? I'm going to starve to death if I have to eat his cooking all the time.

"Come on, Andy. I've called you three times."

I don't want to have to go upstairs and eat with him. If he thinks he can just drop me off at the side of the road anytime he wants to, I don't want him as a father. "I'll eat down here."

"No, dinner isn't TV time."

Sure it is, in lots of houses I've lived in. People practically live in front of the TV. I almost never ate in a real dining room at Weird Joan's or the Morrisseys'.

"Come on," he says, "turn it off." He still sounds mad about having to come get me at school today. But I don't care—I'm mad too, at teachers and kids who don't know anything about adoption. I'm going to watch my movie a little longer.

"Andy!"

"What?"

"Dinner. Turn off the TV and come up."

"I'll come up when I'm ready."

Uh-oh, here he comes stomping down the stairs. He switches off the TV, but I've got the remote and I can turn it on again. He switches it off. I turn it on again. This is fun.

"Andy! Leave it off!"

Who's he shouting at? I just want to watch TV during dinner. Is that a crime? He steps in front of the television to block the signal from the remote. I'll show him. I'll just throw the remote across the room so nobody will ever be able to use it.

"What are you doing?"

Doesn't he know? I'm having a fight with him, that's what. This happens all the time in my other families, with me and all the foster kids. I'm letting him know he can't make me turn off the TV if I don't want to.

"Pick up the remote, Andy."

No way. I'll throw the power pack to my radio car across the room too. Then he'll see a dent in the wall. Oh crap, here he comes, jumping on me and twisting my fingers to give him the power pack. I'll never open them. I'll never open them . . . all right, take the stupid thing. Just . . . "Get off me!"

"Calm down," he yells. He's practically suffocating me with his big body, and he tells me to calm down? I'll stop squirming just to get him off me.

"Okay," he says as he backs away. He's breathing hard, like he's going to have a heart attack. God, hasn't he been in a fight before? "I don't know what's going on here," he says, "but I want us both to settle down now and go up to dinner."

Dinner? Is he kidding? I don't eat with somebody who jumps on me like that. "I'm not coming up." All I have to do is fold my arms and sit here. What's he going to do, drag me up the stairs and stuff the food in my mouth? He better learn he can't scare me. I've already had done to me pretty much everything a kid can go through.

"If you don't come up now," he says, "don't expect any other food tonight. And you better not turn the TV on again or I'll return it to the store."

He goes up the stairs and doesn't look back. I could turn the TV on again, if I wanted to. But the movie is almost over, and I already saw the ending about ten times. I might as well go up. I'm starving anyway, even if it is his crummy food.

She's home now. I can hear her out in the living room talking to Jeff. He'll probably tell her how horrible I was for throwing the remote and getting in a fight with him and all that. Then they'll both be mad at me. It's never good to have both parents mad at you at the same time. I have to act fast, so I run down the hall.

"Hi."

"Andy," she says, "shouldn't you be asleep?"

"I was almost asleep, but then I heard the garage door go up. You're going to read to me, right?"

She looks at Jeff like he should do it, and he says, "I think Andy would rather you read to him tonight, Laurie."

"Yeah, I would."

"Well, I've been working for eleven hours," she says as she takes off her jacket, "and all I had for dinner was a banana and yogurt, so this isn't really the best night for me to read to you."

"Please?" That always gets them. I haven't met a mother yet who can say no to a kid asking to please be read to.

"All right," she says, "but only for ten minutes."

So I run down the hall and jump under the covers. She comes in and sits on the bed. "What do you want me to read?"

I hand her my old copy of *Tom Sawyer*, which is just about falling apart because I've read it so many times.

She opens to the first page and reads. "Tom! Tom! What's gone with that boy, I wonder, TOM?"

I pull Ted out from under the covers and brush his fur. He used to be white as a cloud, but now he's kind of brown. It's better being read to than reading to yourself because you can ask about things you don't understand. Like with *Tom Sawyer*, every page or so there's a word I've always wondered about, like "perplexed" and "switch" and "ruination."

"You know, you could look words up in the dictionary," she says when I ask her.

"Yeah, but it's easier if you just tell me."

I get her to skip a few pages to one of my favorite parts, where Tom picks a fight with the new rich kid in the neighborhood.

"Neither boy spoke," she reads. "If one moved, the other moved—but only sidewise, in a circle; they kept face to face and eye to eye all the time. Finally Tom said: 'I can lick you!'

'I'd like to see you try it.'

'Well, I can do it.'

'No you can't either.'"

I've read this part plenty of times, but for some reason the words sound different coming from Laurie. "What's Tom going to do to him?"

She looks back up the page. "He says he's going to give the other boy a licking."

"A licking?"

She sticks her big tongue out of her mouth and leans toward me. "Yes, a licking! Like this . . ."

Oh, gross—dive, Fleck.

"Licking means give him a beating," she says. "You can come out from under the covers now."

"You're weird," I tell her, but she's also pretty funny too, which I don't tell her. "Okay, read some more."

FIFTEEN

IF THE WORLD were going to end tomorrow, I'd spend all today breaking windows, that's what I'd do. I bet there are a hundred ways to break glass—like with a baseball bat, and a stone, and your fist. I'd save that for last. A minute before the world was going to blow up or whatever, I'd start punching out all of the windows I could find.

That's what I was thinking about in English class when the teacher, Mr. Feinstein, was assigning us to write an essay about our parents—like where they came from generations ago, and all that crap. Then he said that if any of us didn't happen to live with our *real* parents, we could write about whoever we were living with. He looked right at me when he said this, and all the kids turned around to stare at me.

Just like I thought—*everybody* knows I'm being adopted. Laurie probably blabbed it all over. I saw her talking to my principal when she picked me up one day, and now the teachers look at me like I'm this poor little kid my parents didn't want. I'm Andy the Adopted—that's what kids will call me, I know it. It's happened before. Once they know you're adopted they think there's something wrong with you and they don't want to hang around you. It's like being adopted is a disease that's catching. And parents—they don't want you playing with their kids because they're afraid you'll be a bad influence on them. I hate to break it to them, but some of the worst kids I ever met *weren't* adopted.

Well, if they already think I'm rotten, I might as well be, right? That's what I figured when I saw Mr. Feinstein put his wallet in his jacket hanging on the back of his door. Then I happened to be walking past his room between classes, and he wasn't there, but his jacket was. So I lifted a twenty-dollar bill from the wallet and I was gone in a second. Even Dad couldn't have done it faster.

It was pretty funny later on in the lunchroom when he opened his wallet to pay for his food and he didn't have any money. He had to sign an IOU. Me, I had a great lunch. I paid for pizza for my whole table. Guys I didn't even know were coming up and slapping me on the back.

I thought I was getting off clean, but then Principal Jones calls my name over the loudspeaker and tells me to come to his office. All the kids whistle when they hear that.

So I grab my schoolbag and take the long way to the office, past the gym where the eighth-grade girls are playing basketball. I could hang out there all day watching them, but the gym teacher waves me away and slams the door. When I get to the principal's, I can't believe it—Jeff is sitting there. They sure work fast in this school. It would have taken them all day to get my mom in.

"Sit down, Andy," the principal says. He puts his big hand on my shoulder, and I hate that 'cause I've seen his hands and they're covered with hair. They look like paws. "Now, Mr. Sizeracy," he says, "I was explaining that we have had a bit of a situation today—worse than Monday, in some ways. I'd like to go over the facts."

"What are the facts?" Jeff says.

"Mr. Feinstein, our English teacher for the last ten years, had a twenty-dollar bill in his wallet this morning, and it's missing. At lunch, Andy bought pizza for a dozen boys, and he paid with a twenty-dollar bill."

Boy does he have it wrong. It was sixteen kids altogether, and there were plenty of girls eating too.

"So, my question to you, Andy, is this: Did you take the money from Mr. Feinstein?"

Is he crazy? Dad never pleaded guilty in his life. He always says to make them prove it. "I didn't take any stupid money. Can I go now?"

"You admit, though, that you had twenty dollars at lunch?"

"Sure, so what? Can't a kid have twenty dollars?"

Jeff touches my arm. "You didn't have twenty dollars when you left for school today."

"How do you know? Maybe I did."

"Did you?"

Think, Fleck. You didn't even have a dollar this morning because you begged him for money to buy a Sprite. He'll remember that. You have to come up with a reason for having the money. "No, I found the twenty dollars here, in the hall. What am I supposed to do when I find money? Put it in the lost and found box for some other kid to grab?"

The principal starts pacing back and forth in his crummy little room. If he's such a big deal, why do they stuff him in here? Even the nurse has a bigger office. "I'm going to ask you again," he says, "and I want you to think about your answer very carefully. It's one wrong to steal money but two wrongs if you lie about it. Now, did you take the money?"

I've heard that one before—two wrongs don't make a right. But Dad says two wrongs can get you out of trouble sometimes, if you stick to your story. "I told you already—no. If I stole twenty dollars, would I be stupid enough to wave it around in the lunchroom?"

He can't answer that, so he turns to Jeff. "Mr. Sizeracy, Andy was seen outside the door of the English room—"

"Outside the room?" Jeff says. "Not inside, or coming out?"

"That's right," the principal says, "outside, but—"

"A lot of kids must walk by that room every day."

All right! Old Jeff is taking my side. This is great. Time to sit back and watch the principal squirm.

"Well, yes," he says, "but Andy was the only one who had twenty dollars in the lunchroom. Let's be realistic—Mr. Feinstein had twenty dollars in his wallet, it's stolen, and Andy turns up with the twenty dollars."

"With twenty dollars," Jeff says, "not necessarily *the* twenty dollars."

He's right. There's no way Jones can prove that the twenty dollars I had came from Mr. Feinstein. It's not like it was a marked bill or anything.

"It's circumstantial evidence," Jeff says, "and it's hardly conclusive. Andy has told you how he came to have twenty dollars. Perhaps the bill slipped out of Mr. Feinstein's pocket in the hall, or maybe somebody else took it and dropped it there. I don't know."

"Well, then," Jones says, and I can tell he's given up the argument, "I think it's best if you take Andy home with you now."

That sounds great to me. There's still most of seventh period to go and all of eighth. I'm free as a bird.

On the way out we go past the English and math classes. I give a little wave to the suckers who have to stay inside for another hour and a half. This must be what it feels like to be let out of prison early.

Jeff gets in the Saab and starts driving without saying a word to me. We go a few miles like that. I can't tell what he's thinking. Maybe he really knows I took the money and he's mad at me. For an adult, he's pretty hard to figure. "So," I say, just to feel him out, "you really told off Jones."

"I didn't tell him off, Andy. I just stood up for you because I believed you."

"Wow, you really did? Nobody ever believed me before. I thought you were smarter than that."

He slows down and looks over at me. "You mean you took the money from your teacher's wallet?"

Uh-oh, I should have kept my mouth shut. I guess I might as well admit it now and just act like it's no big deal.

That sometimes works. "Of course I took it. Even butt-face Jones knows that."

"Don't talk like that."

"God, every kid says 'butt-face.' It's just calling him a name. Adults call people different names all the time, so kids should be able to use their own words, right?"

"Andy, listen to me. I believed you. I thought Mr. Jones was unfairly accusing you. How do you think that makes me feel now to know that he was right, that he knows you better than I do?"

I've never had anyone get this upset over me lying before. Mom and Dad lied all the time, and I heard most of my foster parents say stuff that wasn't true.

"Andy, I asked you a question."

"What was it again?" I'm hoping he'll forget the question and just watch where he's driving.

"I asked you, how do you think it makes me feel to know you lied to me?"

"I didn't think of it as lying to *you*, okay? I was lying to the principal."

"You shouldn't lie to anyone," Jeff says, "but especially not to me—if you want me to be your father."

SIXTEEN

MY IQ REALLY is 123, like I said before. I didn't believe it either, at first. The doctor who tested me told Sylvia, my first foster mom, that he was very surprised because 123 is superior. I guess he figured I'd be dumb just because my mom and dad never went to college or anything. You don't have to go to college to be smart. Jeff read a story at the dinner table about the richest guy in the world, and he dropped out of college after, like, a year. Me, I don't want to go for even that long, so maybe I won't be the richest kid in the world. But I'll get by.

The thing is, when you're smart you don't want to do dumb things. Like going to the supermarket. I mean, it's Sunday afternoon and Laurie says she needs my help shopping. What did she do before I came—pay some kid to go with her? I'm going to look pretty lame buying groceries with a mother.

When we get there she waits for me to get out of the car and waits for me walking across the parking lot and waits for me inside the store. I can't stand it! "Just go on, will you? I'm coming." That gets her—she turns down the bread aisle and walks away. I'm on my own. I hate new stores 'cause

you never know where anything is. Like, where's the chocolate syrup and the pancake mix and ice cream sandwiches?
Where's the potato crispers and barbecue chips and pop
tarts and honey roasted peanuts? It takes me ten minutes
to find everything, and then I have to run around the store
looking for her. I should have known—she's loading up in
the vegetable section.

"What's all this?" she asks when I dump my armload
into her basket.

She must be blind. "Food."

She picks up the pop tarts and starts reading the ingre-
dients. "Sorry, I can't buy this. It's just sugar masquerading
as a breakfast food."

This is terrible. Is she going to read every stupid ingre-
dient on every stupid box? I have to come up with a good
argument. "All the kids eat pop tarts. I'll get up every morning and eat breakfast if you have them."

"That's the problem," she says. "You'll eat it in the
morning and be bouncing off the walls all day at school."

"No, I won't. Sugar doesn't do that to me."

"You told us it did before—remember when I was baking cookies the day you moved in?"

Yeah, I remember, but I won't admit it to her. "I can't
remember that far back except for important stuff and that
wasn't important so I didn't try to remember it."

"Well, that's what you said."

Usually mothers will buy me anything I want in the
market. I know how to wear them down so they're practically begging me to go get more pop tarts—if I just stop

bugging them. Laurie is tougher than I thought. It's time for me to get tough. "Fine," I said and grabbed the box of pop tarts from her. "I won't eat this or anything else for breakfast. I'll just starve myself, and then we'll see how I do in school."

"Okay," she says, "that will be up to you."

"Yeah, okay, it will be."

"That's what I said."

"Well, I'm saying it too." Finally she gives up and pushes the cart down the aisle. I got the last word.

But I'm still holding the pop tarts. I don't like people walking away from me like that. Who does she think she is? I can walk away too, and she'll be sorry because then she'll have to look for me. So I head the other way down the aisle and toward the door. Some guy in a white jacket comes running over and asks if I'm planning to buy the pop tarts. I check my pockets, but there are only a few pennies left from Mr. Feinstein's twenty dollars, so I have to hand over the pop tarts. They're strawberry too, my favorite.

Now what I am I supposed to do? I could just wait for her at the car, but that's not much fun. Besides, it's starting to rain. So I find a hiding spot behind the fence separating the post office from the parking lot. From there I can look through the slats and watch for her when she comes out.

She takes forever. She's probably hunting up and down the aisles for me. Finally she comes out with a cart full of bags. It's so heavy she has trouble steering it to the car. Serves her right. She's looking all around as she goes, looking for me. I figure I'll let her load the car, then I'll just cruise on over and ask her where she's been, like I've been looking for *her*.

She packs the trunk with the groceries and shoves the cart into the return area. It's time for Fleck to show himself. I sneak around the fence and duck behind some cars so she won't see where I've been hiding. She's checking all around the parking lot now, and I have to keep crouched down so she won't see me. This is funnier than anything. When I look back up, she's getting into the Saab. In a second, she's pulling out of her parking spot. Then she's gone.

I can't believe it. Mothers aren't supposed to leave their kids like that. I could run after her, and maybe she'd see me in the rearview mirror. But I'm not going to run after somebody who doesn't want me.

God, what do I do now? I don't even know where I am. I should have watched how she got here and then I could hitch a ride back home. I don't even have a quarter to call anybody.

Dad always said: Don't panic. Use your head. My head says that what I need is money so that I can call Jeff and tell him I'm lost. I might even start crying a little. Maybe then he'll yell at her for being so rotten to me.

It's raining harder. I'm going to get soaked standing out here in the parking lot just because Laurie couldn't wait five more seconds for me. The cars are all locked, of course. Nobody trusts anybody in this town. There's a Honda and Jeep and Ford Explorer and another Honda—all locked. Then this big fat car pulls in a few spaces over. A lady gets out and runs toward the market holding a paper bag over her head to keep from getting wet. I don't think she took the time to lock her car, and when I wander over, I see that I'm right. I open up the driver's side and slide behind the wheel just like I belong there. It feels good being in a fancy car like this with leather seats and a CD player. This is living. I figure the woman won't be back for a few minutes, so I take my time looking for money. The glove compartment, side pockets, ashtray—nothing. Then I look under the mats and around the seats—still nothing. All I need is one lousy quarter. I should get out, but the rain is pouring down now and it's fun shifting and steering. I could drive this car, I bet. It doesn't look hard. So I'm fooling with the wipers and turn signals and everything else there is to touch, and a little drawer pops open full of change. Bingo! as Dad used to say. There are enough quarters in here to call California, if I wanted to. I take the one quarter that I really need and a second one in case I drop the first one, and then a third one because sometimes the pay phone eats your money. Three quarters should be plenty. It's time to find a phone.

I get out and see a police car turning into the parking lot, its blue light flashing. They can't be coming for me, right? Please, God, please make them be after somebody else and I'll be good for . . . the rest of the week. I really will. Please, just this once, help me get out of a mess.

Don't run, Fleck. Just hurry a little toward the market like you want to get out of the rain. Crap—the car's pulling right up alongside me with two cops inside.

"Hold it, son."

Son—why does everybody call me that?

"What's your name?"

I don't have to tell them that. I don't have to say anything. I know my rights.

"Cat got your tongue?"

I figure a little crying might help, so I start sniffing and wiping my eyes with my shirttail. One of the cops reaches in his pocket and pulls out a handkerchief, but I'm not touching that.

"We got a call about a boy breaking into a car in this lot. That wouldn't by any chance be you, would it?"

The cops in this town are really dumb—fast, but dumb. Do they always ask their suspects if they're guilty?

Just then the woman who owns the fancy car comes out of the market and points at me like I'm on the Most Wanted list. "That's him," she says. "I was coming back to lock my car, and I saw him get in."

"Okay, partner," the cop says to me, "let's go over to the station."

I could run away from them, but Dad says the time to run is before they get a good look at you, not after. So I let them put me in the back of the squad car and take me to this little brick police station. They keep asking my name and where I live, but I shut up and won't tell them anything. One of the cops sends out for pizza and soda. I know it's a bribe, but I eat it anyway. "Now, how about telling us your name?" he says. When I shake my head, he shakes his and takes my arm. "Okay then, we can't spare a man to watch you all day, so you'll have to sit in our cell until we find out who you are."

A real prison cell—wait till the kids at The Home hear about this! The cop locks me in and goes back down the hall to the front desk. I'm alone, and it's kind of scary. There's a metal toilet on the back wall, right out in the open. I'd never go in that, where anybody could see me if they walked by. I'd rather blow up. There's nothing else in the cell except a sink and a bed that's hard as a rock. I lie down on that, and it doesn't take me long to understand what Dad says is the worst thing about being in a little jail—it's boring. In a real prison they probably have TVs and games and stuff, but here there's nothing. The only thing to do is close your eyes and dream you're someplace else.

"Hi, I'm Laurie Sizeracy, and I'm looking for a boy twelve years old."

At the sound of her voice I jump to my feet. I can just barely see her at the front desk down the hall.

"I'm his . . ."

My what?

". . . his legal guardian."

Just like I thought. She won't even say I'm her son.

"Well, it just so happens I have a boy about that age in the back, kind of a skinny kid, brown hair, doesn't talk much."

"That sounds like him," she says, "except for the not talking part. Where is he?"

"In our holding cell."

"In a cell?" She sounds like she can't believe it. What

does she think, I've never been in a jail before? I visited my dad. This is nothing. He could bust out of here in a minute.

"We didn't want to put him there," the cop says, "but he wouldn't speak to us, wouldn't even tell us his name. We didn't know if he was a runaway or what. We thought he might bolt for the door when we weren't looking, so we locked him up. It was either that or cuff him to the bench."

"Can I see him?"

Okay, Fleck, here comes the big scene. They're coming to get me.

"Let's go, son," the cop says. I can hear him unlocking the cell door. Then he pokes at my leg like Jeff does in the morning to wake me up. "Your guardian's here."

"I'm not going anywhere with *her*. She left me in the parking lot—she didn't tell you that, did she?" There, that should tell her off. I bet she's staring at me like she wished she could choke me—I've seen that look before on mothers. Maybe she'll go crazy right here and try it. Then the cop can be a witness and they'll lock her up instead of me.

"Well, sergeant," she says, "apparently he doesn't want to come home with me. I guess you'll have to keep him here until you can reach his social worker. That will probably only be a few days, if she's not too busy with other boys."

"No problem," the cop says, and he puts his key back in the cell door and locks it. "We'll take care of him until then."

What's going on here? They must be pretending. They wouldn't really keep a kid locked up overnight, would they? I mean, the mattress doesn't have any sheets or blankets, and then there's the toilet right out in the open.

"Of course," he says, "we don't usually have juveniles in here overnight because it gets pretty dark in the cell, and there's only one officer on duty, way up front."

"Do your best, sergeant," she says and starts walking away.

Another step and she'll be out the door. "Wait!" That stops her. She turns around and stares at me. She knows she's got me, and there's nothing I can do. "Okay, I want to come home. So you can unlock the door now."

The cop doesn't move. He looks to Laurie.

"Why should I want you back," she says, "if you don't want me?"

Because Al placed me with you, that's why. You're supposed to want me even if I don't want you. That's the way parents are supposed to be. Why doesn't she know that?

"Maybe I will want you," I tell her. "Maybe I just need more time."

She looks at the cop and nods. That means she's going to take me back. I knew she wouldn't leave me in jail.

SEVENTEEN

MONDAY'S THE WORST day of the week, because what do you have to look forward to? Five days of school. But today is different because it's a holiday. I don't know which holiday and I don't care. I just know I have the whole day free.

I would have slept till noon except for Tiger. I was having this dream about riding my bike off a cliff that was so high I was sailing through the clouds. I think I saw this on a commercial once. Anyway, in my dream I pulled the cord to open my parachute, but nothing happened. I dropped through the clouds and I was falling and falling—then something grabbed my foot. I woke up and it was Tiger! I shook her off, but as soon as I moved my foot a little she pounced again. She would have chewed my toes off if I hadn't pulled her away. She meowed at me like, "Why are you stopping my fun?" So I gave her a big kiss on her nose. Tiger is my kind of cat.

But my dream is ruined, because you can't go back to sleep and get to where you left off. I'll never know whether my parachute opened or I crashed into the ground. Maybe it's better I woke up because Dad told me that if you dream you die, then you really do die in your sleep. I wonder how he knows that? I mean, if you don't wake up, how are you going to tell anybody what you were dreaming right before you died?

I jump out of bed and listen for a moment, but I can't hear anything. The house feels empty. Where could they be? I walk across the hall to the bathroom and there's Jeff's razor out on the sink next to a can of shaving cream. I don't have any fuzz on my chin yet, not like José, but I figure I might as well see what shaving feels like. So I spray out some foam and spread it over my face like I saw Dad do. Then I take the razor and . . .

"Hey, Andy, what are you up to?"

I just about slit my throat from being surprised, seeing Jeff in the doorway. He's standing in his bare feet—that's why I didn't hear him coming down the hall. "Nothing," I tell him, which I know is pretty stupid since he caught me red-handed.

"Trying out shaving?"

"I wasn't hurting anything."

"Just don't press too hard with the razor against your face," he says. "I put a new blade in this morning, so it's very sharp."

That's strange. He doesn't care that I'm using something of his without asking. My other foster parents would be yelling at me for being inconsiderate and sloppy and who knows what else. He just leaves me there to shave, like I'm really old enough.

For some reason they've both been pretty nice to me

after all the trouble I've been getting into. Of course, they made me apologize to my principal for lying to him and my English teacher for taking his twenty dollars. Mr. Jones kept nodding his head, like "I knew you did it." That was irritating. Jeff's keeping my allowance each week until I have enough to pay Mr. Feinstein back. And Laurie made me go to the police station to tell the cops I was sorry for causing trouble for them.

I don't mind any of that. Those aren't real punishments, not like getting whipped with a belt like my dad used to do to me. A belt can really hurt, especially on your bare legs. One time he swung the buckle end at me, but Mom saw him and took it away from him. I can't remember what I did wrong that time that got him so mad. It didn't take much when he was drinking.

Parents are interesting. I always thought they were all the same, that they all yelled at you even when you didn't deserve it and punished you just because they *could* punish you. Some of my foster parents didn't even say what I did wrong sometimes, so how was I supposed to know not to do it again? I guess they didn't think it was any use teaching me. I guess they thought I'd never change.

Jeff and Laurie are different. They're always explaining stuff to me. I complain about it a lot, but at least I know they think I'm smart enough to learn.

I figure I should try to be good for a while. I could even do something for them. So when I finish shaving, I put all of Jeff's things back exactly where they were. I head out to the kitchen looking for something nice to do and see Laurie sitting on the back deck reading. I open the refrigerator to grab some grapes, and while I'm looking in there an idea comes to me—I'll make her lunch.

The only thing I really know how to make is a greasy cheese sandwich, so I pull out the Muenster, butter, bread and I'm on my way. I do everything very quietly—get out the frying pan, make the sandwich, turn on the stove, and fry the greasy cheese. In three minutes it's done perfectly, except for being burned on one side. I put that on the bottom. Then I pour her a glass of milk and head out back.

"Andy," she says, "I didn't know you were hungry already. I would have made you lunch."

"It's not mine. I made it for you. Here."

I hold it out to her, but she doesn't seem to get the idea. "For me?"

"Yeah, I made you lunch. Don't you want it?"

"Well, milk and . . ."

"A greasy cheese."

"Right, your special sandwich." She puts down her book and sits up straighter in the chair as she takes the plate and glass from me.

I wait until she takes a bite, and when I see the cheese dripping from the bread I start wishing I'd made one for myself. "How is it?"

"It's a greasy cheese all right. Thank you for making me lunch, Andy. That was very nice of you."

"I know . . . I mean, thanks for thanking me." Then I'm off to do my next nice thing. I'm going to wash Jeff's car. I've never done that before, but I've ridden through a car wash so I know you just throw on the soap, rinse with water, and dry it off. That doesn't sound hard.

Jeff left the Saab parked in the driveway when he came back from the store this morning, which is perfect. I tell them I'm going downstairs for a while and then sneak out to the garage. In a minute I find all I need—a hose, some rags, a sponge, a bucket, and laundry soap. I hook the hose up to the sink in the washer room and turn on the water. Then I drag the hose through the garage and out into the driveway. It's a hot day, so I take off my shirt to catch some sun. When I open up the nozzle on the hose, the water bursts out against the side of the car and sprays back on me. I never knew washing a car could be fun.

I pour detergent into the water in the bucket and then throw the whole soapy mess onto the Saab. I rub it in with the sponge and spray again with water. After that I dry off the car with the rags. The whole thing takes me only ten minutes. This is easy, and the Saab looks better than . . .

"Andy!"

I turn around, and there's Jeff standing inside the garage, at the door to the washer room. Water is flooding over his feet.

"What are you doing?"

"I'm, I'm . . ." What's the use explaining? I'm making a mess of things, as usual.

Staying out of trouble has always been tricky for me. My shrink at The Home said trouble is like a bad friend who keeps whispering in my ear, "C'mon, Andy old pal, there's

no harm in trying something different. Have a little fun."
He said I had to stop listening to this bad friend inside
me. I tried not to laugh at him, but I couldn't help it. I
mean, he was talking to me like I was some little kid. I told
José about this and he said his shrink says the same thing
to him.

My shrink was wrong. I never hear voices in my head
from my bad friend or anybody else. It seems to me that
trouble just happens to me. I'll turn the corner and there
it is, staring me in the face. In that case, my shrink said, I
should just turn around and walk the other way. The thing
is, I've never been good at walking away from an interesting situation, and trouble is interesting.

Like fighting. In fourth grade my school started me
in counseling with a therapist named Dr. D'Angelo. She
shook her head at me a lot. If there was a fight going on,
I was usually in the middle of it and ended up being sent
to Dr. D. I learned how to fight from Dad, and I was so
good at it that little kids would pay me to get bullies off
their backs. I charged five dollars. Nobody liked fighting
me, even the bigger kids, because they knew they'd have
to kill me before I'd give up. Even if I lost I'd always get
my kicks in. Sometimes I couldn't remember who I was
fighting for. Dr. D. told me there was never a good reason
to fight, and I said, "What about the Revolution and World
War II? Weren't there reasons to fight then?"

"That's different," she said, which is how adults always
answer when they don't have a good answer. I didn't make
too much progress with Dr. D. She left for another school

after a few months, but I don't think it was totally to get away from me.

Being good can be awful boring. If you think about it, being good means doing everything the way somebody tells you to or expects you to. If every kid was good all the time, you might as well have little robot children running around. What's fun is doing something different, something that nobody else would think of doing.

I'm going to eat worms!

The reason is this: After we mopped up the washer room Jeff showed me how to attach the hose to the spigot so that water wouldn't leak all over the floor. He said that there was no real harm done, but I should always ask before I try something like that. He said that he'd been meaning to wash the Saab, so I had done him a favor.

Then he asked me to "have a catch" in the yard. Dad always said we were "playing catch." Anyway, Jeff was throwing me grounders and pop-ups, and then I'd whip the ball to him as if he was the first baseman. But every other play he stopped and ran over to show me how to bend my legs so the ball wouldn't go through them and how to hold my hands so I wouldn't miss a fly ball. God, can't a kid just play a little catch without being taught something every second? That's what I told him after about the hundredth lecture on why I had to keep my hands together. He still kept at me, so I threw down my glove and sat right there in the grass in the middle of the yard. He came up and asked me what the problem was, like he didn't know. He was the problem! I was really trying to be nice too, but he wouldn't stop telling me how to catch the ball. My dad never cared how I did it, so why does Jeff?

He finally went in the house and that's how come I'm sitting here now with a clump of grass in my hand, thinking about eating worms. A couple of brown wrigglers, about three inches long if you spread them out, are dangling from the dirt. They don't look very tasty. One thing I've learned is this: If you're going to do something nasty, you have to just do it fast. You can't think about it for too long. So I tell my hand to take one of the worms and stick it in my mouth. I bite off half and start to chew. It tastes slimy and salty, kind of like the oysters Dad made me try once. I swallow fast and then stuff the rest of the worm in my mouth. After a little chewing, I swallow that, too.

I don't really want to eat any more, but it seems to me that most any kid could eat one. But eating a second worm after you know what the first one tastes like—how many kids would do that? So I pick out the longest, thickest, squirmiest worm and take a bite.

The back door slams shut. When I look up, there's Laurie running across the grass shaking a wooden spoon at me. "Andy, don't eat dirt!" she shouts. "Spit it out!"

"Not dirt," I manage to say as I swallow. "Worms." I hold up the wiggling half in my fingers to help her understand.

"That's worse," she says. "They'll make you sick."

I lie to her then without even thinking I'm going to. It's a habit I picked up about a year ago when I discovered that lying makes situations a lot more interesting than they are on their own. "I've eaten worms plenty of times before and never gotten sick."

Her eyes widen, like she's looking into some dark room. "Well," she finally says, "if every boy ate worms, there wouldn't be any left for the birds, would there?"

"Guess not, but I don't think most boys will be eating worms."

"You're right," she says, "especially twelve year olds. I might expect it of a six year old."

I put the half-worm back in the grass and cover him with dirt. My tongue still feels slimy, and I scrape it between my teeth and let drop a big glob of brown spit.

"Here, this will clear your mouth," she says, holding out the wooden spoon, and I lick off the batter. The taste is awful sweet.

After the excitement of eating worms, I feel like a bike ride. So I set off on Hawthorne, standing on the pedals to pump up the hill. At the top I see the wooden mailbox with the birds on it that I whacked. I hop off to check it out, and it looks good to me, the way Jeff and I fixed it, better than new.

Then I hear a little tapping behind me. When I turn around, there's this old man crossing the street, rapping his cane in front of him. This must be Lucinski. He looks kind of like a bulldog with short legs and a neck as thick as his head.

"I know you?" he says.

I shake my head.

"Then what in tarnation are you doing at my mailbox? Filching my checks?"

"What's that mean?"

"Filching means stealing—don't they teach you anything at school?"

"Yeah, I know a lot. And what would I want your stupid checks for anyway?"

"Stupid checks, are they?" he says and swings his cane at my legs so that I have to jump out of the way.

"Hey, watch it."

He's squinting at me now through his thick black glasses. "I never forget a face," he says, "and I know yours."

I turn my bike around to leave because this guy's giving me the creeps, but he sticks his cane in the spokes of my wheel so I can't move.

"You're that boy who knocked off my mailbox a couple of weeks back, aren't you?"

"What if I am?"

He huffs at me. "You think it's enough your daddy dragged you to my house to make amends? You aren't man enough to do it by yourself?"

"I'm not a man. I'm just a kid."

"So you're not old enough to know better?"

"I know better."

"Fine," he says. "Then I expect you'll be wanting to say you're sorry to my face, with no daddy around."

I don't want to say it, but I might never get away from this guy if I don't. "Okay, I'm sorry I busted your mailbox. How's that?"

"You don't sound very sorry."

"I am. I'm very very very sorry."

He nods at me and pulls his cane out of my wheel. "You've made things right now," he says. "You can go."

Who does this old guy think he is, bossing me around like this? I'll show him. "What if I don't want to go?"

He huffs at me again and pulls his letters from his mailbox. "Suit yourself. You can stand out here till you sprout some sense for all I care." With that he taps his way slowly across the road and is gone.

What's the worst thing Laurie could make for dinner tonight? Macaroni and cheese! I couldn't believe it when she put the plate in front of me. And then she gave me two big spoonfuls of string beans. It all looked like worms to me.

I couldn't eat. Jeff said I had to sit at the table anyway. So I had to watch them crunching slithery string beans and juicy little pieces of macaroni. I told them I felt sick. She said that's what I get for eating worms.

Now it's nine o'clock, and I just want to sleep or read, but my dopey English assignment is due tomorrow— Describe Your Family Tree. I don't have a family tree. I have family weeds, and who wants to write about them? This is what I've written so far:

My father is a thief. He's not even a good thief because he gets caught all the time and sent to jail. We used to visit him there, and I hated that.

My mother has babies and then gives them to relatives because she doesn't like taking care of them. She gave me up too, but not when I was a baby.

I don't belong to them now. I don't belong to anybody. I used to go to a shrink and he said I'm like a puzzle piece flipped over and some day I'll flip back and fit in with a family. But I don't think I'll ever flip over. I'm going to have to make every other piece flip over, like me.

There, that's My Family Tree, and I don't want to write any more about them. What I want to do is go to sleep. The only trouble is my stomach. I don't think it knows what to do with the worms. It kind of feels like they're still alive inside me. Maybe they're crawling into places they shouldn't be. Laurie wanted to take me to the emergency room this afternoon to see if they should pump my stomach. But Jeff said the worms would probably pass through me by tomorrow without doing anything. I sure don't want to see what they look like when they come out.

I've put away my homework and brushed my teeth really hard. I even brushed my tongue. I said good night to Jeff and Laurie, so I'm ready to read. The thing is, I can't stop thinking about the worms inside me. It's like in that old movie I saw once, *The Village of the Damned,* where the teacher is trying to blow up a schoolroom full of blue-eyed alien kids who can read minds. He walks into the class, talking to them as if everything is fine, but the kids can tell he's nervous. They radar in on his brain and see that he's thinking of a wall. That starts them wondering—why would anybody be thinking of a wall? They zoom deeper into his thoughts, and finally the guy can't stop himself from thinking of the bomb inside his briefcase. But it's too late for the little aliens—the bomb explodes, killing them all.

So I'm trying to think of every other thing in the world except worms. But no matter how hard I try, it's WORMS that keeps popping into my brain. I remember them dangling from the dirt and then my hand stuffing them in my mouth and my teeth chewing them. Every time I swallow, it feels like another worm is sliding down my throat. I pull the pillow over my face, and I'd smother myself if I could. I open my mouth and take a big bite of the pillow. It feels dry and clean on my tongue. Then I reach to the bookshelf and grab the closest book—*Frankenstein!*

EIGHTEEN

TEACHERS SAY YOU can never do enough reading. But I think I did too much last night. I read *Frankenstein* till midnight, by flashlight under my covers.

It's a terrific book. Everybody thinks Frankenstein is the name of the monster, but he's really the scientist, Victor Frankenstein, who invented the monster. I don't think the monster should be called a monster, either. He couldn't help being big and scary looking. That's the way he was created. He tried to fit in and make friends, but people attacked him. He didn't want to hurt anybody.

Anyway, I'm dead tired this morning. They've been calling me for a half hour to get up for school, but my body won't move. Laurie has been threatening all kinds of punishments if I don't get up RIGHT THIS MINUTE. Every time she says that, I sink further into the mattress. The doctors say I have "oppositional disorder," which means I hate to do what somebody tells me to. So why aren't they smart? Why don't they order me to stay in bed and *not* go to school? Maybe then I'd jump up, eat breakfast, and get out to the bus stop on time.

"Andy, this is your last chance. Get up now or you'll lose all your privileges this afternoon when you get home."

Big deal. There's nothing to do around here anyway. The kids in this neighborhood are all a lot smaller or bigger than me. There are no bike trails nearby or ballfields, or even a parking lot where I could skateboard.

"I'm counting, Andy—ten, nine . . ."

All right, I'll get up. I can't sleep anyway with her yelling at me from the hall. My alarm clock says 6:45, which means I have ten minutes. That's plenty of time to pull on some clothes, grab a mug of orange juice, and brush my teeth. Here goes Andy into high gear . . .

I reach the door with a minute to spare. No sweat.

When she opens it, I can see this little rain falling. You'd have to look through a magnifying glass to see it.

"It's pouring," she says. "Don't forget your jacket."

A jacket? I'd look like such a geek. She probably wants me to take an umbrella too. "I don't need any jacket."

She opens the closet and pulls one out. "Yes, you do. You'll be soaked."

"I don't care."

"I care," she says.

She won't give up. I have to make a run for it. I push out the door and I'm halfway across the yard, with her on my heels. "Take it," she says and throws the jacket over my shoulder. Why can't she leave me alone? I swing around to get the jacket off me, and my elbow kind of slams into her nose. I didn't mean to do it—I never hit a girl before. But it serves her right for butting into my business. A kid should be able to decide if he needs a jacket or not.

The bus is coming down the street, and I run toward it. I'm not going to look back.

Ever notice how fast the day goes when there's something rotten waiting for you? It seems like I just left the house five minutes ago. But here I am on the bus going back, and now I'll have to face the music, as Dad says.

I know they're going to kick me out. She's been waiting for an excuse, and now she has it. I really was just trying to get the jacket off my back. How did I know her nose would be sticking out so far when I swung around? It's not my fault she put her face where it shouldn't be.

I don't want to go back to The Home. I just left there not even two months ago. The kids will rag on me for busting out of another place. It could be next year before Al finds a new family to take me. I'll have to go through more of those awful adoption parties where you feel like an old cat at a pet store when everybody's picking up the cute little kittens. I can't help it that I'm not cute anymore—I'm twelve years old! Maybe Al won't ever find another family for me and then what? I could die in The Home.

Maybe the bus will flip over at the turn and I'll bash my head in. I'd have to go to the hospital, and then they couldn't yell at me, right? Come on, bus . . . crash. Crash! Why couldn't Ed drive like a maniac like some I've had? He's creeping along at ten miles per hour. We'll never flip over going this slow.

Here comes Hawthorne. Ed turns and pulls over to the curb. The other kids hurry to get out. I'd hurry too, if I were them. Maybe if I duck down he won't see me and I could sleep all night in the bus. The next morning when they find me I'll say I fell asleep and got locked in and it was horrible but I'm okay and I just want to go to my wonderful bedroom at home and sleep for a while. Jeff and Laurie couldn't be mad at me if that happened, could they?

"Last stop, Andy. Everybody out."

Ed doesn't miss a thing. All right, Fleck, get off the bus and walk across the yard like you're not worried. Never show them you're worried. It feels like walking the plank in those old pirate movies where they make the bad guy step right into the ocean. Think. I got to think.

There's the door opening. I knew it. They're both waiting for me. I feel sick . . . wait a second. That's it! Hold your stomach and run to the door. "Please don't throw up. Please don't throw up. Please don't throw up."

"Andy, what is it?" he says as I push inside. He takes my schoolbag off my shoulder and I close my eyes like I might faint. Steady, Fleck, don't overdo it.

"I'm okay . . . it's just . . . my stomach."

"Do you feel like you're going to throw up?"

"Maybe. I don't usually throw up. But after lunch I started feeling sick. I think it was a rotten carrot, but I'm not sure."

"The worms," she says. "That's what it is."

"Yeah, the worms. I was okay until we hit this big bump on the way home, and then I almost hurled."

"We better get you into the bathroom," she says, which gives me a chance to take a peek at her face. Her nose looks the same to me as before. I don't even see a bruise. I must not have hit her very hard.

They hurry me down the hall like I might throw up any second and splatter the walls. They shut the door behind me, but I know they're listening in the hall. So I moan and gag a little to make it sound real. Then all I have to do is flush the toilet and kind of stagger back out into the hall.

"You okay?" Jeff says.

"I'm not sure."

"Let's get you into bed." He takes me by the arm to my bedroom and pulls down the covers. I kick off my Nikes and crawl in bed.

Then Laurie comes in with a green plastic pail in one hand and a bottle of pink medicine in the other. "We'll put the pail next to your bed," she says, "in case you have to throw up and can't make it to the bathroom."

"What if Tiger jumps in there and I have to throw up? Should I do it on her?"

Laurie laughs at that, and I think maybe it's the first time I've ever made her laugh. "You better yank Tiger out of there first," she says. Then she pours some of the pink stuff onto a spoon and aims it at my mouth. "This will settle your stomach." I hate taking medicine, especially when I'm not even sick. I don't have any choice, though. I open up and she sticks the spoon in my mouth. The stuff tastes nasty, just as I thought. "Get some rest now," she says and straightens the blanket over me.

When she leans over the bed, I whisper, "Sorry about this morning."

She looks at me for a moment, as if she isn't sure she heard right, then smiles.

NINETEEN

ON THURSDAY, AT exactly 2:29, I'm watching the big red second hand on the English room clock moving toward the twelve. Mr. Feinstein is going on and on about when to say "bring" and when to say "take." I already know that—*bring* with you, *take* away. That's easy. It seems to me everybody always understands no matter which word you use, so what's the difference anyway?

Five, four, three, two, one . . . where's the two-thirty bell? What happened? The principal fall asleep or something? This isn't fair. They shouldn't be keeping kids in . . . All right! There it is, the bell! I'm outta here.

Everybody's running into the halls and banging into each other, but I don't care 'cause I'm running and banging them too. I have to get to the bus line first so I can sit in the back. That's where the skater kids sit, and I think I could get to know some of them if I just play it cool, like I don't really want to know them.

I take the shortcut through the cafeteria and then push through the big double doors to the outside. The bus is just pulling up, so I could be first in line. Then from behind me someone says, "Hey, buddy, how's it going?" I know this voice, and it stops me cold. When I turn around, I can't believe what I'm seeing—Dad! He waves me over to the side of the school, out of the way of all the kids. "So," he says, leaning over me and putting his hands on my shoulders, "you've gotten bigger."

"Maybe a little bit, but I'm still pretty small."

He shakes his head. "I'd say you look pretty tall for ten years old."

"I was ten when they took me away, Dad. I'm almost thirteen now."

"Sure you are. That's what I meant to say."

The kids coming out of the school look over and see Dad with his hands on my shoulders. They probably think he's some pervert trying to get me to go with him in his car. That's what he looks like with his messy hair and black beard. And why is he wearing his red and black hunting jacket when it's so hot out?

"So how are you doing?" he says.

"Okay."

"Your new family treating you good?"

"Pretty good."

"They must be rich, living in a town like this."

I shrug at that, 'cause I don't really know if they're rich or not. They're richer than any other family I've been in, that's for sure. But they don't seem very rich next to most of the other houses in town.

"I was wondering," he says, "if you could help me out."

"Help how?"

"I just got out of jail, you know, and they don't give you

any money to get you back on your feet. Your mother wouldn't take me back into the apartment, so I'm kind of on the street."

So that's what he's come for—not to see me, but to get money from me. That sucks. "How is she—Mom, I mean?"

"Doing better than me, that's for sure. I could really use a few dollars."

"I don't have any, Dad. They took away my allowance last week." I pull out the pockets to my shorts to show I'm not lying.

"But your new parents have money, right? They wouldn't miss a few dollars. You could get one of their wallets for me."

Lots of times Dad told me about holding up 7–11 or the video store, and he made it sound exciting. He made it sound right too—everybody else had money, why shouldn't we? Now it just seems strange to hear him talking about stealing like it's an okay thing for a father to do.

"I don't think they carry much money around, Dad. They're always using credit cards."

"That's all right," he says. "I can use their cards for a little while before they realize they're gone."

I don't want to do this. But how can I say no to Dad with him standing there looking like some homeless guy, begging me to help him? Besides, I've heard Jeff and Laurie talking about giving money to the poor, so why shouldn't I help Dad? He's poor.

"Tomorrow afternoon," he says, "I'll be parked up the street from your house an hour after school lets out. You bring me a wallet, okay?"

I'm used to doing what he says, and I nod to him without thinking. I guess that means I'm going to steal for him.

"So, anything interesting happen at school today?" Jeff asks me at the dinner table.

I keep my head down as I take the bowl of applesauce from him so my face won't let on my secret. Dad says I'm lousy at poker because I always give away whether I'm bluffing or not. "Nothing much. Just the usual."

"*Something* must have happened," Laurie says, and that makes me wonder, did they get a call from school saying a strange guy was hanging around me? Are they just trying to see if I'll admit it was Dad?

"I can't think of anything," I tell them. "Could I have some more of the green stuff?"

She goes to the kitchen to get the pan from the stove. "You must really like broccoli," she says as she spoons it onto my plate.

"Yeah, I must." To tell you the truth, broccoli makes me gag just thinking of it. But I'll do anything to get them to stop asking me questions.

"Well, how about telling us something you learned today?"

Won't she ever give up? I have to throw them a curveball. "I bet you don't know who had asses' ears."

"Andy, you don't need to talk like that," she says.

"No, I swear—I mean, I'm not swearing, I'm serious. It's somebody from thousands of years ago."

"Who's that?" she says.

"Midas the king. He always wore a hat to cover his ears because they were like asses' ears and he didn't want anyone to know. Except his barber knew, and he had to keep it a secret or Midas would kill him. One day the guy couldn't stand keeping his secret any more so he ran out of the castle and dug a hole and yelled into the ground, 'King Midas has asses' ears.'"

"Not so loud, Andy."

"Oh yeah, sorry." I'm stuffing the broccoli and rice and rolls into my mouth while I'm talking, because the faster I eat the sooner I can get away from the table. "The barber thought he was safe doing that, but the weeds grew up and every time there was a wind the weeds called, 'King Midas has asses' ears,' and all the people heard."

I pick up the last bit of broccoli and cram it into my mouth. There, my story's done and so am I.

"You told that very well," Jeff says. "It's one of my favorite myths."

"Thanks," I say and take my plate to the kitchen. "Since I told you something I learned, can I go to my room now?"

She says no and he says yes. I decide to listen to him. I run down the hallway and shut the door behind me. Then I set myself to thinking how to do what Dad told me—steal a wallet for him tomorrow.

TWENTY

DAD SAYS YOU have to be light on your feet to be a thief. And always keep your eyes open so you're ready when the perfect opportunity presents itself. There's only a half hour till I'm supposed to meet him up the street with a wallet in my pocket, so there's no way I can wait for a perfect opportunity. I have to steal now.

Jeff's sitting at the dining-room table with his books and papers spread out. When I came home from school he didn't ask me to have a catch with him out back, so I know he's working. That means he won't be paying much attention to me.

It's strange. Even though I weigh about a hundred pounds less than Dad, I'm not as light on my feet as him. He could sneak up on a squirrel, which I saw him do one time. The floor in the hall squeaks a lot, so I turn on the radio in my room to cover my noise. Then I creep into their bedroom.

It's scary and kind of exciting being somewhere I'm not supposed to be. I could be caught any second. I keep telling myself—You have to do this, you have to do this. Don't let Dad down!

My hands are shaking as they open the top drawer of Jeff's bureau where I've seen him put his wallet sometimes. There's nothing but socks. I look in his night table, but there are only a few pads and pens.

Then it comes to me. Whenever I've been out with him in the car and he stops for gas, he always reaches into the door pocket for money. That's where his wallet might be.

I whistle my way down the hall, take a sharp turn at the steps, and head down to the playroom. Then it's through the washer room and into the garage. I figure I'm far enough away from Jeff now that I don't have to worry much about making noise. I just open the driver's side door of the Saab, and there's the fat leather wallet sitting exactly where I figured. Dad would be proud!

I look inside it and there are a bunch of twenty-dollar bills folded up—I can't tell how many—and a half dozen credit cards. That should be enough to hold him for a while.

I'm ready to go, but then I see a little picture of Jeff sticking out from one of the pockets. I pull it out and it's his driver's license. "Jeffrey Elwood Sizeracy"—Elwood? That's the funniest middle name I've ever heard. I'll have to razz him about that. There's another picture. I pull that out and I can't believe it—it's me! He's carrying around a picture of me holding Ted in my bed. I remember him taking it a couple of weeks ago. I wasn't going to smile, but he told me to say "cheeseburger," and I couldn't help it.

Can I really do this? It's terrible having one dad who's asking you to steal from another dad. How did I end up in the middle?

I put everything back in the wallet the way it was and head back to the washer room. I don't know what to do. If I don't take the money, Dad might come after me at school again. He'll be really mad that I disobeyed him. If I do take the money I'll be hurting Jeff. But maybe he'll never know it was me. Maybe he'll think he made a mistake at the bank.

The door to the playroom suddenly opens, and there he is, standing at the other end of the washer room. I whip the wallet behind my back fast.

"What do you have there, Andy?"

"Nothing."

"Let me see what nothing is."

I can't believe he followed me down to the garage. A father is supposed to trust his son, isn't he? "You were just waiting to try to catch me at something, weren't you? You don't trust me."

"At this moment," he says, "you're right. I don't trust you."

"Then . . . then tough!" Before he can stop me I run out the back door, hop on my bike, and I'm off to meet Dad.

He's waiting at the top of the hill, just like he said. I've never seen this car before, a beat-up Chevy that looks about a hundred years old. I ride up to the window, and he's taking a big swig from a carton in a brown paper bag. "Right on time, buddy," he says and wipes white stuff off his lips—milk. Dad got hooked on it the summer he was trying to give up beer. "Did you get me a wallet?" he says. I hand it over and he empties out the cash. "Good boy—you did good for your old man."

"Yeah, but Dad?"

"What?"

"He kind of saw me."

Dad wheels in his seat and looks back down the road. Then he starts the car.

"Wait, Dad . . ."

"I have to go, buddy."

"But he saw me. I can't go back there now. What am I going to say?"

He puts the car in gear, ready to go. "Say anything you want—just not my name." He hands me the wallet. "Here. At least you can give him his credit cards back."

"But Dad, I thought maybe I could come with you."

He gives me a strange look, just like when he caught

me one time talking to Ted as if he were real. "Are you crazy? You don't need a father who spends half his life in prison. You got it made right here, Andy, if you don't screw up." He reaches out and takes my arm. I think maybe he wants to give me a good-bye hug or something, but he just moves my arm off the car and speeds away.

Now what? Maybe I should just do what Orange the cat did and take off on my own. The thing is, how far can I get on a junky old bike and no money? They'd catch me in a minute and throw me back in The Home. I could just go tell Jeff the truth about Dad and all, but *he* didn't take the wallet, *I* did. Besides, he is my dad, no matter how bad he acts. I don't want to get him sent back to prison. He'd never forgive me for that.

So here I am sitting on my bike at the top of Hawthorne Road. There's a path into the woods across the street, next to old man Lucinski's, and I wonder where that goes? It's getting colder, and I'm just wearing a T-shirt and shorts. I should have planned for staying out longer. Where's Jeff anyway? He should be coming in his car by now, looking for me. I mean, I stole his wallet. For all he knows I was trying to run away. Doesn't he care?

I guess I should go back, hand him his wallet, and tell him I'm sorry. I didn't want to steal from him. But Dad asked me to. A kid's supposed to obey his father, isn't he?

I know stealing's wrong. Even Dad says that, and he should know since he does more of it than practically anybody. But he says he can't help himself. He says stealing's in his blood. And he says his blood runs in me too.

Like father, like son. But if Jeff's going to be my new father, then I should be like him, right? I'm not planning on spending my life behind bars, that's for sure. One hour in the smelly Concord jail was enough for me.

I need time to think. Across the street is Lucinski's driveway, which goes past his house and right up to his barn. I figure I could stay out of sight there for a while without him knowing it. So I walk along the grass next to the driveway, not making any noise. I sneak past the house and I think I'm in the clear. Then a voice just about scares me out of my sneakers.

"Going somewhere?"

There's Mr. Lucinski sitting in a folding chair inside his screen porch. He's wearing a heavy sweater and a cap pulled down low on his forehead. The stub of a cigar is sticking from his mouth.

"I was just . . . just . . ."

"Come on, boy," he says, and the cigar bobs between his lips, "you must be quicker at making up stories than that by now."

It seems to me that it's not worth the effort trying to fool this old guy since he doesn't believe anything I say. I lay down my bike and walk up the steps so I'm just on the other side of the screen from him. "I'm sort of running away because I did something wrong, and I was thinking of doing it in your barn for a while."

"You mean you did something *else* wrong?"

"Yeah, something else."

"You have an interesting life, don't you?" he says and

then reaches out with his boot to push open the screen. "Come on in and we'll talk about it."

I know I shouldn't go in the house alone, especially with somebody as strange as Mr. Lucinski. But he's so old he couldn't do anything to me. Besides, he might even give me something to eat.

He goes shuffling down the hallway and I follow along behind him. I have to hold my nose 'cause the whole place smells like cigar. He turns into a room with a bare bulb hanging from the ceiling. It's about the dimmest bulb I've ever seen. I can hardly see him.

"How come you keep it so dark, Mr. Lucinski?"

"Light costs money, boy. What do you think, they give it out for free?"

In the corner something moves—an old dog raising its head from a giant pillow. It sniffs the air my way, then goes back to sleep.

"You say you ran away?"

"Sort of."

"What's that mean?"

"I wasn't planning on running away. I just went out and got in trouble, so I was thinking it might be better if I don't go back. But I might—go back, I mean."

He grunts at me. "That man who brought you around before, is he really your father?"

"Sort of."

"How come everything's *sort of* with you?"

"I don't know. It's kind of complicated."

"Well, you live with him, right?"

"Right."

"So he's acting like your father whether he is or isn't. I guess he'd tan your hide good for getting in trouble again."

I try to imagine Jeff taking his belt off or slapping me, but the man in my imagination looks like Dad, not Jeff. "He wouldn't do that."

"He could lock you up in his cellar and never feed you, couldn't he?"

"He did threaten to send me to bed once without dinner."

"That's what I mean," Mr. Lucinski says.

"But he didn't do it. And he wouldn't starve me. I know that."

"So let me get this straight. You're sure he's not going to whip you or starve you, right?"

"Right."

"The worst he'll do is yell some and make you stay in, right?"

"Right."

"And that's exactly what you deserve, isn't it?"

"Yeah."

"So why are you afraid of going home if you're just going to get exactly what you deserve?"

When he puts it like that, I don't know.

The ride down the hill takes only a minute. I lean the bike against the wall along the driveway and let myself in the house. It's very quiet. You wouldn't think anything big had just happened here. I go upstairs as quietly as a cat, and there's Jeff standing in the kitchen talking on the phone.

I figure he's calling the police on me. He turns around when he hears me, says something into the phone, and hangs up. Then he puts his hand out toward me. He wants the wallet.

"Is the money all there?" he says as I give it to him.

I shake my head.

"How much is gone?"

"I don't know exactly—I guess everything that was in there."

"What happened to it? You didn't have time to go anywhere and spend it."

I shrug because what can I say? Unless I tell him about Dad, he'll think I hid the money somewhere to use later.

"I had sixty dollars in here, Andy. Where is it?"

"I can't tell you."

He's staring at me like I'm the rottenest kid in the world for taking his money. That's how I feel too. One of my shrinks told me that it was a good sign that I feel rotten when I do something wrong. It shows I have a conscience. Sometimes I think it would be easier living without a conscience.

"I'm waiting for your answer, Andy."

"I didn't take it for myself, okay? That's all I can say." I turn and start down the hall to my room, but he comes after me and grabs my arm.

"We're not done talking. What do you mean? Who did you take the money for?"

"I said I can't tell you."

"That's not a good enough answer."

"It's the only one I have."

"All right, go to your room," he says like he's punishing me. I mean, that's where I was heading in the first place. "We'll talk about this later."

That's fine with me. I always like dealing with things later, any time except now.

TWENTY-ONE

"LATER" TURNED OUT to be when Laurie came home
for dinner. I heard the garage door go up and then Jeff
going downstairs to meet her. He probably told her everything. Now they're upstairs trying to figure out what to do
with me. I know the routine. It always ends up the same,
with me being moved back to The Home or some foster
place with a million new rules to learn and new parents to
get used to. I hate going to new places.

I've stayed in my room all afternoon, like he told me,
and I think I've come up with a pretty good reason for why I
took the money. I'd believe me, if I was them, but you never
know about parents. Sometimes they believe the stupidest
reasons you give them. Other times they don't even believe
the truth.

They're talking in the hallway now, coming toward my
room, and then there's the knock on my door.

"Who is it?"

They don't answer. They just come right in. "Andy," he
says, "we have to talk."

It's never good when parents say "we have to talk." I
need to get them thinking of something else before we get

to the wallet. "I want to get my ears pierced, okay? All the kids are wearing earrings, you know, so I'd fit in better." He puts up his hand for me to stop talking, but I have to keep going. "Earrings aren't just for girls. They used to be, but not now. Pirates wore earrings—you know why?"

"Andy, we're not talking about pirates right now."

"The reason is that they kept them from getting seasick. I don't know how, but it must be true because José read it in a book."

"Not everything's true that you read in books," she says.

"Not even the ones we read in school?"

"Andy!" he shouts at me, "We can talk about pirates and earrings later."

"Okay, you don't have to yell."

She pulls out the chair to my desk and sits down, which means this is going to be a long talk. He walks back and forth across the room. "You know that I saw you come out of the garage with my wallet, Andy. I saw you run away with it, and then you gave it back to me with sixty dollars missing. I want to know where my money is."

"I told you—I gave it to someone."

"Why would you give away sixty dollars?"

I rub my hand over my eyes so they'll look red. "Because . . . I couldn't help it . . . there were three of them . . . they were going to beat me up if I didn't." Terrific—here comes Tiger walking in my room. She jumps right up on my bed and into my lap.

"Some boys were going to beat you up if you didn't give them sixty dollars?"

I nod, but I know that sounds like an awful lot of money. "They didn't say sixty dollars exactly. They wanted twenty, but a car was coming and they got scared and grabbed the wallet and took all the money. Then they threw the wallet back at me."

"Who are these boys?" she says.

I knew she'd ask that. "One of them was Joe. I know that 'cause I heard them call his name, but I never seen—"

"—never saw," she says.

"Yeah, I never saw them before."

"Then how did you know they wanted money from you?"

Hmm—good point. "What I mean is I never saw them before yesterday when I was out riding, and they knocked me off my bike and told me to come back today with the money or else—"

"Andy," she says, "are you telling the truth?"

I cross my heart and hold my hand up like I'm in a courtroom taking an oath. "Sure, because I wouldn't take money from you—that's wrong. My first dad takes money. That's why he's in jail so much. I don't want to go to jail like him." I know this is what they want to hear—that I don't want to be like Dad. It's true too. I don't want to have to steal things all the time just to live.

"Well," Jeff says, "we're going to have to call the police about this."

Police? "No, you can't do that."

"Andy, this isn't just some kids taking your lunch money. It's sixty dollars."

"But they'll kill me if you tell the police. They really will. That's what they said."

"They're not going to kill you, Andy."

"They'll beat me up, that's for sure. You want me to come home some day with my face bloody and my arm broken and my teeth knocked out?"

"And your nose broken?" she says. "Maybe your ribs cracked?"

I think she's kidding me, but I figure I should play along. "Yeah, that too. And my ears cut off—I think they said they'd do that."

"Then you wouldn't have any place to put your earrings." She's making a joke again, and I don't understand. Why isn't she acting really *really* angry at me? I stole from them.

"This is serious," Jeff says to her.

"I know," Laurie says, "but we don't have to act like he killed someone. Maybe Andy can learn something from this. When you steal and lie," she says to me, "you lose a person's trust. It's very hard to get that back. People will always wonder, is he going to steal from me again? Is he lying again?"

Nobody ever talked to me about trust before. It's strange to have a parent explaining stuff like this. My dad used to just yell and swing his belt.

Laurie gets up from her chair. "Andy's had a lot of years of learning the wrong things," she says to Jeff. "I think we should start today teaching him something right and give him another chance. But it was your wallet, so maybe you don't agree."

They look at each other, and they seem to be talking without using words. It's like they have a secret way of communicating.

"I'd like to trust you again, Andy, but I need you to trust me with the truth."

The truth—that I'm a thief like my dad? That I lie like my dad?

"I'm your dad now," he says, "and I expect you to act like my son."

He's right. He is my dad now, and I hope he's my *last* dad. My first dad took off running with the money and left me to explain. I don't owe him anything. Being like him just gets me in trouble all the time. I might as well try being like Jeff.

"Okay, well, the thing is, I was lying about the kids making me give them money. It wasn't any kid. It was my dad."

"Your dad?"

"Yeah, he came up to me after school yesterday and asked me for money. He was practically homeless, you know, so I was trying to help him."

"Help him by stealing—that was his idea?"

"Yeah."

"Andy," Jeff says, "your dad gave up his rights as your father. He isn't supposed to have any contact with you. I want you to tell us if he comes around again, okay?"

"Okay."

"He put you in a difficult position, but still, you're old

enough to say 'no' when someone tells you to do something wrong. So you're going to have to pay back all the money."

"Yeah, I will, every cent. I can mow the lawn or whatever you want. And you can take my whole allowance after I get done paying back Mr. Feinstein—except it would be nice if you left me two dollars a week. That way I wouldn't bug you all the time for money when we're out. You could keep the rest till I make sixty dollars."

"It's also important that you never steal from us again," Laurie says, "or from anyone."

"No, I won't."

"We don't want to have to hide our wallets or lock up the cars," Jeff says. "We're going to trust that from this moment on, you're not going to take anything from us, no matter what reason you think you might have."

I cross my heart and swear on Tiger that I won't steal for the rest of my entire whole life. She starts purring in my lap, and then it hits me what I've just done—sworn on my cat's life. I really can't steal ever again.

Dad wouldn't understand, but I don't care. Like Al says, it's my life. I have to decide what kind of kid I'm going to be. It's not easy, but I think I'm starting to figure it out.

TWENTY-TWO

TODAY'S THE FIRST day of the rest of my life.

I didn't make that up—I saw it on a bumper sticker. If you think about it, though, every day is the first day of the rest of your life. What I mean is that today is the first day of the rest of my life without stealing.

"Let's go, Andy," Jeff calls down the hall to me. "Don't forget your glove. There's a softball game."

We're going to a picnic. Mrs. Freed—I mean Joanne, the woman who gave me the yo-yo—is having a picnic at the ballfields for the Science Explorers Club. At first I didn't want to go because I'm not an Explorer and the kids are all probably younger anyway. Also, I hate picnics. The ones I've gone to were actually adoption parties. You think you're going to have fun playing games with the other foster kids, but there are all of these parents looking you over. It's like they're at a deli checking out the meats in the glass case before picking what they want.

I know this won't be anything like that. Laurie told me there would be lots of food and music and games with prizes. That sounds good to me, so I grab my cap and glove and I'm ready to go. But halfway down the hall she sees me. "Hold it, Andy. Not that T-shirt."

"It's my favorite, from Bonkers."

"This is the first time you're going to meet some of our friends," she says, "and I don't want them seeing you in a shirt where the boy's banging his head on the wall."

Sometimes you can tell with a parent that there's no use arguing. So I go back to my room and dig to the bottom of my drawer for a blue T-shirt with nothing on it, front or back. When I turn around, she's standing in my doorway. "Is this boring enough?"

"Perfect," she says.

The center of Concord is full of fields for soccer and baseball, and there's a track, a swimming pool, two basketball courts, and swings. Why haven't they brought me here before? Kids are running all over the place, and some of them I recognize from school.

"See," Laurie says, "I told you there would be boys and girls your age here."

Jeff and I head to the softball game, and they put us in the outfield. There's not much to do out here because the little kids can't hit past the pitcher and the men who come up blast the ball over our heads. Jeff picks a long blade of grass to suck on, so I do too.

I pretend to catch a fly, keeping my hands together the way he showed me, and when the ball hits my glove I fire it all the way to home plate. The runner's out!

"How did you like my throw?" I ask Jeff.

"Very nice," he says. "Let me try." He shades his eyes with his glove, runs around a little, and at the last second throws his right arm out to catch the ball. Then he winds up a few times and pretends to throw home—with his left hand. That's strange.

"You're left-handed?"

"Yep, I am."

"I never knew anyone left-handed before."

We hear the crack of the bat and look up, but the ball's heading to right field, not center. I pick another blade of grass to suck on and start thinking about how it would feel being left-handed. "If I started eating left-handed and throwing left-handed and everything else, do you think I could make myself left-handed?"

"You'd certainly get good at doing things with your left, but you wouldn't change your natural hand."

"Are dogs and cats right- and left-handed?"

"You mean right- and left-pawed?"

"Yeah."

"I don't know," Jeff says, "but I read once about some lobsters being left-handed."

"You mean left-clawed, don't you?"

"You're pretty smart," he says. "You know that?"

Yeah, I always thought I was smart, but it's cool to have someone tell you.

After a while it's our turn to bat, and I'm up. The first pitch is slow and high. I figure I can slam this one for a home run easy. But when I swing, I hit nothing but air. The second pitch is just like the first, and I'm sure I'm going to clobber the ball out of the field. I hit nothing again. This is sure harder than mailbox baseball.

Jeff comes around the screen and puts his hands on my shoulders like I'm lame. I feel pretty stupid, but I know he's just trying to help. "You're trying to murder the ball," he says. "Swing easy. Just make contact."

"Okay, now go back, will you?"

The next pitch is faster, and I foul it into the screen. At least I hit something. Then comes another slow, high pitch. I wait and wait and then swing easy. The ball hits my bat and takes off like a rocket. I can't believe it.

"Run, Andy, run!"

Oh yeah, I forgot about that. I take off toward first base, and some guy on the side waves me to keep running so I head toward second. Everybody's cheering and I can't tell where the ball is so I run toward third. Jeff's standing behind the base yelling "Slide! Slide!" so I dive headfirst at the bag. I guess I don't really know how to slide because my face smacks into the dirt. I feel like I just ran into a wall. When I open my eyes I see the bag is a couple of inches in front of me. I stretch out and touch it—I'm safe!

"Andy, are you okay?"

Jeff picks me up off the ground and I reach up to check my face—my nose is still in the right place, so I feel great. "I swung just like you told me, Jeff. Did you see it? That was my first triple ever. Next time I'll get a home run, I bet."

"Next time," he says as he dusts me off, "try sliding feetfirst."

After the game I run to the picnic tables to tell Laurie about my triple. Before I can say a word she puts her arm around the woman next to her and says, "Andy, you remember Mrs. Freed."

Mrs. Freed . . . Joanne. "Oh yeah, you gave me the yo-yo."

I put out my hand to shake, but it's covered with dirt, and Laurie grabs it. "Your palm's bleeding," she says, "and the side of your face—it's all red, like a brush burn. What have you been up to?"

"That's what I'm trying to tell you. I was swinging really hard and missing everything, and then Jeff told me to swing easy so I did that, and the first pitch I fouled off and the next one I hit about a mile. So I ran around the bases and I was coming into third and Jeff yelled 'Slide,' so I did, headfirst."

Laurie takes a bottle of water from the table and pours it over my hands, then gives me paper towels to dry off with. "Looks like you ripped your shorts too," she says, pointing at the right pocket. "I didn't think softball was this dangerous."

"A triple is a pretty special thing," Joanne says. "Not everybody can do it."

"I bet some guys go their whole lives without hitting a triple."

"I think you're right," Joanne says. "Now how about some lunch for the big hitter?"

I'm not really hungry, but when she puts it that way, sure. So I squeeze into a place at the picnic table, and people are coming and going. I grab a few potato chips and drink some grape juice. Then Laurie hands me a plastic container full of potato salad. What am I supposed to do with that? I pass the potato salad to the woman next to me, who says, "Thank you." So I say, "You're welcome." Laurie hands me a plate of coleslaw. I pass that on and the woman says, "Thank you." I say, "You're welcome." When I look around again Laurie's holding an ear of corn over my plate. Before I can stop her she drops it from the tongs. When she turns away I hand my plate of corn to the woman next to me and she says, "Thank you very much." I say, "You're welcome very much."

"Andy," Laurie says, "you need to eat something. There's ice cream later, *after* you eat lunch."

"But I don't like anything so far."

She reaches into the big food box and pulls out a huge bowl of red stuff. "At least have some Jello." She scoops out three large chunks with a spoon and plops them on another paper plate. The Jello shakes a little, as if it's alive. It smells great, but I'm not touching it. I lean over and whisper so just Laurie can hear me, "I can't eat this."

She pulls away from me. "It's not polite to whisper in front of people, Andy. Mrs. Freed made the Jello especially for you kids."

"But—"

"No buts. Cherry's your favorite flavor. You have to eat something, so eat this."

I stick my spoon into the Jello and pull out a little bit. Laurie's loading up her plate with potato salad, but I know she's watching me. Joanne's sitting right across the table, and she's cool. I can't be rude to her. I have to eat. I close my eyes, raise the Jello to my mouth, and suck it down fast.

I can't believe it—I just ate pig skin! Don't they know where gelatin comes from?

"Pretty good, isn't it?" Laurie says. "Make sure you finish all you've taken."

All *I've* taken? I put another little spoonful in my mouth and swallow fast. It really does taste pretty good. If only José hadn't told me what it's made from, I'd love eating Jello.

TWENTY-THREE

MY SHRINK AT The Home told me that all kids test their parents, but adopted kids do it more. Sure we do. A regular kid grows up with his parents and knows how much he can get away with before they'll really punish him. And the punishment is always something like grounding him or sending him to bed early. An adopted kid doesn't know what the limits are. There's always the chance that if he crosses the limit the punishment will be getting kicked out of the house.

Today I'm testing to find out whether Jeff will make me get up and go to the dump with him, like every other Saturday. We have to load the car with newspapers and cardboard boxes and plastic bottles and tin cans for recycling. Then there are bags of garbage that smell worse than a skunk. I don't like going to the dump, but I've always gotten up before.

"Andy, I've been calling you for a half hour," Jeff says as he stomps down the hall again. "I need you to get up."

"Okay." It really confuses parents when you say "okay" to them but then don't do anything. They can't yell at you because you haven't said no. They can only go away and come back in ten minutes, like Jeff does.

"You said you were getting up, Andy."

"I am. Soon."

"Now, Andy." He reaches over and taps my shoulder. "Andy?" Now he's trying to pull off my blanket, but I have it tucked under my fists. "Come on, I need you to help me." He swats at my legs. That doesn't hurt, but I don't like it anyway because Dad used to hit me there. Jeff whacks at my legs again. Why's he keep doing that? I'll give him my karate kick.

"Watch it," he yells and backs away.

"You watch it," I tell him and duck under the covers. I don't hear anything. I think he's trying to trick me into coming out. But I won't look. Then I feel his hands grab the blanket off me. "Hey, what are you doing? What if I was naked?"

"Get up," he shouts, but he doesn't scare me. Dad is scary—not Jeff.

I pull the blanket back over my face. But he yanks it so hard he practically tears my hands off. My Walkman goes flying across the room and crashes to the floor. He broke my Walkman! And it's the last present Mom ever gave me. "You ruined it, you butthead. You ruined it."

"Don't call me that, Andy."

"You're going to buy me a new one."

He picks up the pieces and tries to put them together, but he doesn't know what he's doing. "You shouldn't have it in your bed anyway," he says. "You're not supposed to be listening to music after lights out at night. Here," he says and hands me back the Walkman, "see if it works."

I'll see if it works all right. I take it and throw it into the wall. I don't want it anyway. What good is it for a mother to give you a dumb old Walkman if you're never going to see her again? Besides, what I really need is a CD player.

"Pick that up," Jeff says.

Oh yeah, like I'm really going to . . . hey, what's he doing? Get off me.

"Pick up the Walkman."

"No, get off me. You can't make me." He's got his big arms around me, but I can still squirm like a snake. He's trying to pick me up. He's slipping his hands between my legs—what's he doing? "Stop it, you pervert. Stop touching me. I'm telling. I will. Get off me!"

When he lets go, I see Laurie standing in the doorway. I've got a witness!

"He touched me where he shouldn't have. He touched me and I'm going to tell Al because you can't be touching kids like that."

"Lower your voice, Andy," she says.

"I was just trying to get him out of bed," Jeff says to her.

"You were touching me all over—you know you did."

"If I touched you, it was an accident."

"Sure, they always say it's an accident. But it doesn't make any difference. You touched me."

They look at each other, and I can tell they're scared. Now they know how it feels. I'm scared all the time of getting kicked out of the house.

I'll call Al and she'll come out and yell at them. Then

they won't be touching me anymore. From now on I have something to hang over *them*.

I wait till later when they're out on the back porch to sneak downstairs and call Al. I should have figured I'd get her answering machine. She's never in her office on Saturday. I have to listen to her whole dopey recording about how I can leave a message or hit some button and get somebody else if it's an emergency and on and on. Why doesn't she just say, "I'm not here. Leave a message." Finally the machine beeps.

"Al? I mean Alison? You told me to call if anybody ever touched me where they shouldn't. Well, he did. Jeff, I mean. So, that's it. Bye. Oh, this is Andy, in case you couldn't tell. Bye."

There, that should do it. Once Al yells at them, they'll have to keep me because I could go to the police and get Jeff in big trouble for touching me. They'll never be able to get rid of me now.

It's eleven o'clock on Sunday morning, and nobody's bugging me to get out of bed. Laurie called me once to tell me to get up if I wanted pancakes, but that was a long time ago, and I wasn't ready yet. They haven't called me in an hour.

I know what's going on. They're letting me sleep to be nice to me because of yesterday. I think I'll just get up and head to the kitchen to see about those pancakes.

As soon as I start down the hallway, I can tell something's different. It's spooky quiet, like in the movies right before somebody jumps out of the shadows. "Hey, where is everybody?"

There's not a sound. Even Tiger's not lying in her favorite spot on their bed. I peek around the wall into the living room and look down the steps to the playroom—no one there, either. I go back into the kitchen for a glass of milk, and there's a note taped to the refrigerator: "Andy, we went to church. Take your Ritalin on the counter, and help yourself to cereal."

Help myself? To cereal? They have to be kidding. I don't make breakfast, especially not stupid cereal. And how could they leave a kid alone? What if there was a fire while I was sleeping?

I open the freezer, but there's no pop tarts or turnovers, just vegetable pot pies. Who could eat that for breakfast? In the pantry, behind the raisins and granola, I find a jar of cashew nuts they've probably been hiding from me. I like regular old salty peanuts better, but this will have to do. God, why did they go to church? They haven't gone yet while I've been here.

The phone rings and I figure it must be them, so I run to pick it up.

"Hello, Andy? It's Alison, I got your message too late last night to talk to you. It sounds like you have something you want to tell me."

"Yeah, he touched me—Jeff."

"Tell me how he touched you. What was going on?"

"I was trying to sleep 'cause I was really tired and he was trying to make me get up and he pulled my covers off and I could have been naked, but I wasn't, and then he grabbed me down there, you know, like a couple of times."

"Grabbed you?"

"Maybe not *grabbed,* but he was like lying on top of me . . . and rubbing me!"

"You realize you're making a serious charge, don't you?"

"You told me to call if that ever happened, didn't you?"

"Yes, okay. Let me speak to Jeff or Laurie now."

"They aren't here."

"Where are they?"

"At church."

"Are you okay there by yourself?"

What's she think, I'm some little kid? "Yeah, I'm fine."

"All right, well, I spoke to them last night after you went to bed, and I'll be talking to Jeff again. We'll see if we can straighten this out, okay?"

"Yeah, see ya."

They come home just after noon—at least she does. I hang around the kitchen in case she asks if I want some pancakes now, but all she says is, "You take your pills when you got up?"

"Yeah, I did, and then I had some cashews. That's all I could find to eat."

"Well," she says, "I'm making salad for lunch. I can make one for you too."

Salad? Nuts for breakfast and salad for lunch—she'll probably try to feed me broccoli for dinner. And where is Jeff anyway? Didn't he come home too?

She makes the salad with mushrooms, raisins, and cheese, then sets it in front of me with a glass of water. I bet meals in prison are better than this. Finally my curiosity gets to me. "Where's Jeff?"

"He had to go into the city." That's all she says, but I can guess what's going on—he has to go see Al, and on a Sunday!

Jeff comes home right before dinner. He steps over my Lego fort in the playroom and says hi in a strange voice, like you hear in those slasher movies where people rise up from the dead. "You want to have a catch?" I ask as he goes up the steps.

He shakes his head and sort of smiles. "Not right now." When I go upstairs I see them in the dining room whispering to each other. I pretend like I'm looking out of the window for Tiger, but they stop talking when they see me.

For dinner she makes eggplant parmesan, my favorite, with rolls and applesauce. He reads a few stories from the paper but doesn't say anything else. When we're clearing the table he says, "Your social worker, Alison, will be coming out tomorrow after school, Andy. I don't want you to be surprised when you come home and see her."

It does surprise me that she's coming all the way out from Boston. Usually she does everything over the phone because she hates to drive. I guess she figures that if she's going to yell at Jeff, she should do it in front of me.

TWENTY-FOUR

I COULDN'T KEEP my mind on my classes. It's hard enough on a normal day, but today I kept thinking about what I'm going to tell Al. José always says if you're going to make stuff up, don't make up too much, because then they know you're lying. I wonder sometimes—if José knows so much about living in families, how come he keeps getting kicked out of them? He's been in more foster homes than me. I asked him about that one time and he said, "That's how I know more about families, because I've been in more." I don't think that makes sense. I think if he really knew about families he'd have stuck with one by now.

Anyway, I'm on the bus riding home. Kids all around me are razzing each other and shoving each other. That's what I'd be doing too, except I have to get my story straight. If I get all tangled up, Al won't believe me and then she'll end up yelling at me instead of Jeff.

Before I know it the bus is stopping across the street from my house. All of a sudden I don't want to go through with this. I know I called Al, but that was two days ago. I thought she'd just yell at him over the phone. I didn't know I'd have to stand up in front of them all and say what happened. I wish I could just stay on the bus and go someplace else where I don't have to make up lies. It's strange, because usually I don't feel this bad about lying. Dad always said there's a real knack to it, that not everybody can lie. To lie real well you have to really want to do it, and I don't right now.

Ed the driver turns around when he sees all the kids get off except me, sitting in the back row. He says, "I've never seen a boy love the bus so much that I have to kick him off."

"You couldn't drive me somewhere else, could you?"

He waves me to come down the aisle. "Where'd you have in mind?"

"Anywhere."

"Trouble inside?" He flicks his thumb toward my house, and I nod. "Well, if you run away from trouble at your age, you'll probably be doing it all of your life. I'd say you'd be smarter to go in and face it right now. Get it over with. It's never as bad as you think."

Boy is he wrong. Trouble has always been worse than I think. "Thanks, Ed," I say as I hop off. For a bus driver, he's pretty nice.

As I walk toward the front door, I can see down to the driveway. There's a strange car parked there, not Al's Buick. Now I don't know what's going on.

I run around to the backyard and duck down until I get under the living-room window where I can listen.

"And where were you at the time?" a man's voice asks.

"Right there," Laurie says.

"You mean you were in the bedroom during the whole incident?"

"No, I was in the kitchen making breakfast when I heard the yelling."

"So you didn't actually see what happened?"

No, she didn't, so she can't say I'm lying unless she lies herself, and I bet she wouldn't do that.

"I didn't have to see. I heard what was going on."

"Okay," the man says, "what did you hear?"

"I heard Jeff trying to get Andy out of bed. Then there was a crash—that was the Walkman hitting the wall, I guess—and I started down the hall. I heard Andy say, 'Stop touching me, you pervert.'"

"What exactly did you see when you got to the room?"

"Jeff was at the side of the bed. Andy was standing on the bed pointing at him and yelling, 'He touched me. He touched me! I'm telling!'"

"What did you do?"

"I told him to quiet down."

"Were the windows open?"

"A little."

"And you didn't want anyone in the neighborhood to hear?"

"That's right. I didn't want our neighbors hearing things that weren't true."

"How did you know they weren't true?"

"Because I know my husband. He wouldn't touch Andy except when he's throwing a fit and needs to be restrained. That's what Jeff was doing—restraining Andy."

"So you didn't see your husband touch the boy at all?"

"Of course he was touching Andy—he was trying to get him out of bed. He probably touched him a lot of places."

Behind me I hear a snap in the grass. When I turn around, there's Tiger coming toward me, meowing away. It's time for her treat. So I grab her off her feet and head up the back deck. I go in the house like I haven't heard anything and turn into the kitchen.

"Andy," Al calls to me, "can you come here?"

"In a minute. I have to give Tiger her Pounce."

They're mumbling to each other now, so I can't hear anything. After I feed Tiger I head into the room and plop down on the easy chair. This could be interesting watching Jeff get yelled at, as long as I don't have to say much. Al's tapping her pencil on the table. She looks pretty nervous. The other guy introduces himself, some name I can't pronounce. I think he's Al's boss. He says, "Do you understand why we're all here, Andy?"

"Sure, because he did that to me, you know, and he's not supposed to, right? So you're going to tell him he can't touch me anymore."

"It isn't that simple," Al says. "You know how we're always talking about your being safe in a home?"

"Yeah, like you don't want me falling on knives or anything."

"We want you to be safe from all kinds of dangers, like being touched. Obviously we can't let you live where you don't feel safe."

Wait a minute—what's she mean by that?

"It's a very serious thing, what you said on the phone to me. That's why I asked Jeff to come into our office yesterday and why we're here today. We have to make sure you're safe."

I don't understand. Of course I'm safe—just look at me. Somebody tell me what's going on. "You yelled at him, right, Al?"

"We've been talking, Andy. There wasn't any yelling. Everybody knows it's not right to touch a child in certain places."

"Okay, so things are fixed now, and I can go to my room."

"Things don't get fixed that easily," the boss says. "It's not clear what happened here—or if anything happened—but you made a charge, and we have to take it seriously. We can't let you stay in a home where there's any possibility of danger like this. That's the policy of the department. We'll take you back to the Brighton Boys Home until we can sort this thing out."

Oh man, this is crazy. My head feels like it's going to burst open. This can't be happening.

"Andy, sit down now and listen, okay?"

No, it's not okay. "I don't want another stupid home. I want . . . I want this home, with them, and Tiger and Ted and the . . ."

"I know you're upset, Andy," Al says, "but you made these charges."

"I made *up* the charges, okay? He touched me by accident because I was kicking and he was holding me down. Then I remembered what José told me, how he got his horrible stepfather in trouble for touching him. I figured I could do that too, so I started shouting stuff and I didn't know it would turn out like this. I just wanted you to yell at them so I'd have something I could use against them if they ever tried to kick me out."

Al takes a deep breath, and so does her boss. They look at each other like they knew all along that I'd made things up. "Well, I'm glad you've spoken up," he says. "We're going to have to think about this for a few days. In the meantime, you'll have to stay at The Home, as I said."

"But I just told you I was lying. You have to believe me."

The boss leans toward me. "A lot of kids take back their accusations," he says, "and sometimes it's because they don't want to get people in trouble or they're afraid of what will happen to them."

"No, that's not it."

"You wanted us to believe you before when you called Alison, didn't you?"

"Yes, but—"

"And now you want us to believe you. You see, you've made it hard for us to know which story is true. That's why we need a few days to investigate."

I knew it would be worse than I thought. That's the way my whole life is. I shouldn't have gotten off the bus. I have to do something. I have to make this guy listen to me. "Okay, I'm telling you, no matter what you say, I'm not leaving here." I look around to find something to hold onto, but there isn't anything, so I just grab him—Jeff. I'll hold onto his arm forever if I have to.

"Andy," Al says.

"I'm not letting go. I mean it. I'm not going to that freaking home again." Oh man, I feel like crying. I hate crying in front of people. "You said this was my last home, remember? My forever family, or whatever you call it. I'm sick of changing places. I want to stay with this family even if they order me around all the time."

Nobody's saying anything. Why isn't Jeff speaking up for me. Maybe it's because of Laurie. She's probably glad to get rid of me. I have to work on her. "Look, Laurie . . . Mom—I'll call you that, see? I know I bust you all the time. I just never had a mother who acted like a real mother before. But I'll try. I really will. I'll be perfect like you want me to. Just don't kick me out."

She reaches for me, and I let her rub my hair even though I don't like people doing that.

"It's not us, Andy," she says. "We're not kicking you out."

"Then don't let them take me. If I was your real kid and made up some stupid story, you wouldn't let them take me, would you?"

Jeff tries to wiggle out of my grip, but I won't let go. "Listen, Andy, DSS can't just forget you ever said these things."

"I'll take back everything. I'll sign a paper saying whatever you want."

"I'm afraid we started the investigation as soon as you called," Al says. She waves a folder full of papers in the air, and suddenly I know how to fix this mess. I let go of Jeff and grab the folder. Now I have the papers and they'll never get them back. Al starts to get up from her chair.

"Don't come near me. I'm going to run out back and I'll bury this folder somewhere. Don't try to follow me, either, because I'll just go deeper in the woods. I'll stay out there till I see your car leave. And if you don't leave I won't ever come in and then maybe I'll die out there and you'll get fired."

Al and her boss look at each other like they don't know what to do. I know what they should do—just go away and leave me alone.

The guy makes a grab for me and I drop the papers. There's nothing to do now except run. Like José says, when things get really bad—run! I run through the dining room and the porch and out the door onto the deck. I'm outside and running and I won't look back. I cut across the creek, and I don't even care that the new Airwalks Jeff bought me are getting muddy. Then I head up the hill and through the trees with the branches whipping against my face. In a minute I'm running almost right into old man Lucinski coming from his barn.

"Lord Almighty," he says, "you trying to knock me over?"

"No . . . no, I was just . . . I didn't see you and couldn't stop and . . ."

"Slow down, boy. Let your brain catch up with your tongue."

I take a few deep breaths.

"Okay, now why are you running so all-fired fast?"

"They were going to take me out of the house and I grabbed the papers 'cause I don't want to leave and they can't make me except they can make me so that's why I ran but I don't have anywhere to run except here."

He scratches his head with his big fingers. "Let me get this straight—somebody's trying to take you out of the house you're living in, and you don't want to go, that it?"

"Yeah."

He nodded. "I know the problem. They tried that with me too."

He starts walking toward his house, so I follow him. "Who tried that with you, Mr. Lucinski?"

He turns on me like he forgot I was there. "What's that?"

"Who tried to move you out of your house?"

"My own flesh and blood, that's who." He lifts his cane and jabs it in the air. "My sons tried to get me out of this house which I built with my own two hands. Wanted to throw me in an old folks home. Imagine me living in a place like that."

"That's what they want to do with me, too—throw me back in The Home."

He gives me a strange look. *"You* in an old folks home?"

"No, a home for foster kids. That's where I was living before. Then they moved me into the house down the street."

He pulls himself up the steps by the railing and opens the screen door. "You coming in?" he says, which doesn't exactly sound like an invitation, but it's close enough. So I run up the stairs and follow him deep inside the dark, spooky house. He walks down the hallway in little baby steps and turns into the same room as last time. The old German shepherd's lying across his pillow, same as before. This time he doesn't even raise his head to sniff. Maybe he remembers me.

Mr. Lucinski reaches under the shade of a floor lamp

and pulls the chain. Then he squints at his watch and taps it and holds it to his ear. "Must be four o'clock by now, wouldn't you say, boy?"

"I'd say so."

He leans on his cane with one hand and with the other reaches into the front pocket of his droopy green pants. He comes out with a chocolate bar, a big fat Snickers. Then he sits down and unwraps it.

"You get hungry in the afternoon?" he says as he raises the bar to his mouth. I nod as he bites into the Snickers. "Me too," he says, "same time every day." He bites off another piece and licks his lips. "Awful good," he says. "Chocolate's my one sin. What's yours?"

I'm watching him eating the Snickers, and I don't know what he's asking me. "My what?"

"Your sin—the bad thing that you shouldn't be doing but you can't help doing."

"Stealing, that's one—at least it used to be. And lying, I do that a lot. I'm kind of lazy too—is that a sin?"

"I suppose it is," he says as he stuffs the last of the Snickers in his mouth.

"I'm obnoxious—everybody says that."

"Are you now?"

"Yeah, and I get angry real fast and want to break things sometimes, like windows."

"Is that about it?"

"I guess so—oh wait, I don't do what I'm supposed to. Like if some adult tries to boss me around, I don't let them. There, that's it."

The old man reaches down to pet the head of his dog. "This here's Last Chance," he says. The old dog lifts his head at his name and yawns.

"That's a weird name."

"It fits him, though. This mangy creature got into so much trouble biting and chasing people they were going to put him down. He was a wild one. They gave him one last chance with me, and he finally settled down."

"Doesn't look like he has much fun now."

"He's over a hundred in dog years—I'd say his fun days are over."

Then a great idea comes to me. "Maybe you could take me in, Mr. Lucinski, because I'm on my last chance too. I'd be no trouble really."

The old man breaks out laughing so hard he starts choking, and I think he's going to fall out of his chair. "That's a ripe one—I need a boy around here like I need a hole in the head."

"You don't have to be mean about it."

"I'm just saying the truth. The truth can't be mean or not mean. It just is."

There's a loud knock at the door, and we both look out into the hall toward the front of the house. "Get that for me, will you, boy?" I shake my head because it might be them looking for me. He mutters at me and gets up and wobbles into the hall.

"Don't tell them I'm here, okay?" I whisper as he passes me.

"There's no use lying and no use running," he says and then pulls the door wide open.

"Mr. Lucinski?"

It's Al.

"I'm looking for a boy who was living with the Sizeracy family down the street. His name is Andy. Have you seen him?"

"He's here," the old man says, and soon Al's standing in the hallway with that look on her face like Here We Go Again. Mr. Lucinski's right—there's no use running. They always catch you.

TWENTY-FIVE

"LOOK ON THE bright side."

That's what they always tell you at The Home. They even put signs up in all the rooms saying that. But where's the bright side in coming back to this place after living in a real home with a real room all to myself? Now I know how Dad felt when he robbed his last 7–11 and went drinking. He said he was flashing a roll of twenties and buying for every-body. The next thing he knew he passed out on the bar and woke up in jail. He said big mouths run in the Fleck family.

"This all you have?" Charlie says as he lifts my paper bag from the backseat of the van and hands it to me.

"Yeah, I'm not staying long." I don't even know what's in here, whatever stuff Alison grabbed for me 'cause I wouldn't go back in the house after she found me at old man Lucinski's.

"Come on," Charlie says, "you can just make dinner."

He takes me in the back door, the same one I left through with Jeff. I turn in the third doorway on the right, my old room, but Charlie's big hand wraps around my neck and pulls me back. "We have to put you in the storage room at the end," he says. "It's the only space open right now."

"But José and me always room together."

"We didn't plan on you returning, Andy. We had to put another boy in there."

"Can't you move him out?"

"Sorry," Charlie says, "it's his room now."

He walks me down to this puny little room that smells like pee and scum because it's next to the toilets. There's only one window that's stuck shut forever and a cot that fills up the whole floor. I bet Dad's been in cells bigger than this.

I toss my bag on the bed and run down the hall and round the post at the stairs and take them by two. I make it to the eating hall by the count of ten, which is faster than I ever did before. Everybody looks up and claps when I come barging through the door, so I take a bow for them. There's Kenny and Lewis and Hawk and Ronny and Jerome and some new kids I don't know. Hank the Hulk waves me to a place at the table next to him, but I head to the other end where I always sit, across from José. He's there, but sitting across from him is this other kid with spiked green hair.

"Hey, José! What's up?"

He looks at me with this weird face, like I'm the last kid on earth he expected to see again. "Hey, Fleck," he says and takes another bite of his hamburger.

I grab a couple of fries off his plate and shove onto the edge of the bench. Green Hair moves down for me, which is pretty nice.

"What happened?" José says. "They kick you out?"

"Naw, the guy touched me, that's all, and I called my social worker, so she sent me here until they figure stuff out."

"Man, you must be happy to be out of there."

"Yeah, I guess." Except sitting here with ten loud-mouthed kids like me, I'm not happy at all. I lean over the table so just José can hear me. "He didn't really mean to do it. It was kind of an accident. He was holding me because I was kicking."

"You busted him with DSS just for holding you?"

"Yeah, then Al came with her boss and they said they had to pull me till they investigated."

José stuffs a few fries in his mouth. He always eats a bunch at the same time. "So's your social worker going to look for another family for you?"

Another family? They better not try that on me. "No way. I'm going back to this one."

"You mean you like them?"

I know why José is surprised. I haven't liked any of the other families I've been placed with. Sometimes I've gotten along with one parent, like Conner. But I've never had both a mother and father who were cool and trying to be nice to me. "Yeah, I like them."

José sticks a fork into his spinach, twirls it around, and then stuffs it in his mouth. "How come?"

"They aren't crazy, that's why. They're just like normal parents who want to have a kid."

"You think they'll still want you?"

"Sure, why wouldn't they?"

José swings his good left arm across the table and punches me in the shoulder, like I'm joking. "Listen, you screw the guy by calling DSS on him, right? So he gets a record for touching, which ruins it for them if they want another kid. And you still think they'll want you back?"

"I told them I made it up. What else can I do?"

José finishes his hamburger in one big bite. I'm waiting for his answer, but for the first time I ever remember, he doesn't have one.

After dinner José and I go back to his room and sit on the beds, flipping baseball cards into his cap on the floor between us. He wins two straight games, but he doesn't seem all that happy about it. When we're picking up the cards he says, "The Worm's gone."

I wouldn't believe it, except José isn't grinning like he usually does when he's trying to fool me. "You swear?"

"I swear. This family with four kids and a big house in Dorchester took him last week."

This doesn't make sense—The Worm's got a family and José's still here and I'm back at The Home.

José grabs his bottle of Brut from the little shelf over his bed. He pours some on his hands and slaps it on his face. José always smells good. Then he sits back on his bed with his legs crossed under him, like an Indian. "The Worm said his new family might want another kid real soon. He's going to tell them about me."

"You living with The Worm? He'd drive you crazy. You'd kill him the first day. I'm the only one who could play with The Worm."

"I get along with him now," José says. Then Green Hair comes in the room and looks at me like, what am I doing on his bed? But it was my bed for a lot longer than his.

"Come on, José, let's go down to *my* room."

"Maybe later," he says, which is strange because he always did whatever I said before. Green Hair puts a CD in his disc player and hands the headphones to José.

"Yeah, later."

Ted!

This is terrible. He's there and I'm here. I'll never get to sleep without him. And what if they throw him out to get back at me? Weird Joan tossed him in the mud one time and Dumb Donald kicked him in the face. I don't think Jeff or Laurie would do that, but who knows?

Okay, Fleck, it's time to grow up. Who needs a teddy bear anyway? Just because it's about the only thing you have that your dad gave you, so what? Your father is a bum who makes you steal for him and then takes off. So why should I care about some old stuffed animal that he won for me at the park? I remember what a shrink told me once, that Ted represented security to me, something I could love that would never desert me. Maybe that's it. But all I really know is that I can't get to sleep without him.

"Lights out," Hank yells down the hall, and that means now because he counts to ten real fast and flips the switch and everything goes dark. Then he runs down the hall, making sure you're in bed. If you're not, he can report you and you have to do extra chores the next day. So I jump under the covers when his footsteps come toward my room.

I feel scared all of a sudden. The Worm's got a home, and José might move in with him. I'd be left here alone. Why did I have to go and ruin things with Jeff and Laurie? I'm always ruining things. If there were a contest for ruining things, I'd win hands down. It's José's fault, really. He's the one who told me about how touching can get somebody in trouble. I should never have listened to him.

Whenever I feel like this, I need something to hold. I grab the pillow from under my head and hug that to my chest, just like it's Ted.

I know she's got bad news. Alison never takes me to the mall unless she's trying to make up for bad news. But right this minute I don't care because we're in the arcade and she's feeding me quarters for Speed Racer and I'm zooming along, bouncing off walls.

"Very good, Andy," she says as my car flips over and I glide on the roof for a while, then flip back again. That's strange—Al hates smash 'em kind of games. Something must be really wrong. So when I cross the finish line I climb out of the driver's seat, even though I have extra time on the game. "Okay, so when can I go back to them?"

Al takes out a pack of Big Red gum and gives me a piece, then takes one for herself. "Before we get to *when*, Andy, there's a question we have to decide—*should* you go back?"

"I already decided that—yes."

"Other people have their say in the matter, and at the moment they're not convinced it's a good idea."

"I thought you always say what happens."

"Most of the time I do, but this is a special case."

"You always make the plan for me and it's supposed to be perfect, but it never works out and this one's good for once and then you pull me."

"I didn't just pull you, Andy—you made a charge we had to take seriously."

"You never took anything else I said seriously. Like when I said Weird Joan was a witch you didn't believe me."

"You're right. I don't always believe you. But this time I have to take you seriously. You have an appointment with Dr. Lilly tomorrow. He'll help us decide."

I can't believe it—I'm seeing my shrink again.

"Ah yes, young Mr. Fleck," Doc says as I plop down on his couch. "I was hoping I wouldn't be seeing you again so soon."

"Let's do this fast so I can get back home by dinner today, okay, Doc?"

"To which home are you referring, Andrew?"

What's he mean by that? *"Home* home—with Jeff and Laurie."

He shakes some paper in the air at me. "First we have to deal with this," he says. "Your phone call to Alison Schwartz alleging inappropriate touching—by Jeffrey Sizeracy."

"He didn't do it—I told them that already. He was just trying to get me out of bed because I was being a jerk, and he accidentally touched me. He didn't mean to."

"Are you sure?"

"Sure I'm sure."

"How are you sure?"

I hate questions like that. "I just know, that's all."

"But when you called your social worker and left your message, and again when you talked to her on the phone, you insisted you were touched on purpose in your private area."

"Yeah, I made that up to get him in trouble."

"Your social worker suggests the possibility that you are making up a different story now to get Jeff out of trouble so you can live there again. How can we tell?"

"I don't know. Why are you asking me? I'm just a stupid kid. I'm telling you I lied the first time and I'm not lying now. That's it! End of story."

"I have some other questions, Andy."

"I'm not answering."

"Well then, I guess the session's over for today," Doc says and spins in his seat so he's staring out of the window.

"Right, I'm leaving then."

"Okay," he says, "good-bye."

"Good-bye."

Al says it could be a week before Doc gives them his report and they have a meeting to decide about me. That's too long. In a week Jeff and Laurie might forget about me or get another kid. In a week the whole world could blow up, and this is the last place on earth where I want to end up dying.

TWENTY-SIX

JOSÉ SAID I'LL never make it. He said nobody who runs away from The Home even gets out of Boston. But I got him to loan me all the money he had in his pocket, which was four dollars, and here I am riding the Green Line to North Station. I've taken the subway alone before. I'm not scared.

I can see from the map above the seats that North Station's the last stop. When we get there everybody piles out, and I just go with the crowd over a little foot bridge and down the stairs toward the trains. This is how Jeff took me home from the ball game at Fenway Park. I know what I'm doing.

Except things are different when you're with a parent. They're in charge of knowing where to go. All you have to do is follow them. North Station is huge and noisy. People are hurrying past me going both ways. I'm looking for a sign saying "Concord," but I don't see any. I start one way, then the other, then back the first way.

"Need help?"

I turn around, and there's a man wearing a black conductor's uniform. "I'm trying to get to Concord. Which train is that?"

"Track two," he says and points to the far end of the station. Then he checks his watch. "You better hurry—it leaves in one minute."

"Thanks."

I take off, and it's like I'm on a football field running around tacklers. I bump into a few people, but I don't have time to say I'm sorry. It's lucky I don't knock anybody over. I get to Gate Two and jump on the train at the first open door. Nobody looks up when I walk down the aisle. Nobody cares that I'm alone.

I drop into an empty row and the train starts moving. After a minute a conductor comes by.

"Where to?"

"Concord."

"One way to Concord, and how old are you?"

"Twelve."

"That's four dollars."

I open my hand with my money in it. After paying for the subway, I only have three dollars left.

The conductor looks at the money. "Are you sure you're not fooling me, sonny? You don't look more than eleven to me, and that's half price."

"Well, I could be eleven."

"Sure, you could," he says as he takes two dollars from my hand and gives me back a ticket. "No use growing up too fast."

I sit back and watch the towns go by . . . Belmont, Waverly, Waltham. Before I left, José said, "Even if you get there, what are you going to do if they aren't home, break in?"

I said, "Yeah," but I don't think it's really breaking in because it's my house too. It's like if you lose your key to your front door, then you'd have to go through the window, right?

"Next stop, Concord!"

I hop out of my seat and hurry down the aisle. When the train stops, I jump out. The conductor's standing on the platform, and I figure I should say something to him, since he let me go for half price.

"You have a very nice train, sir."

"Well thank you, sonny. Come ride with us again."

Now for the walk home. I know it's pretty far because I biked past here a couple of times. It's probably the farthest I've ever walked, so I decide to count each step. In one hundred steps I reach the Dunkin' Donuts. In a thousand steps I'm passing the library. I walk on and on until I get tired counting, and finally I see Hawthorne Road up ahead. I'm home.

Dad showed me once how to break into a house without making a mess. I guess he thought I'd need to know that some day. I don't have a knife, so I find a stick and punch a hole through the corner of the screen in my bedroom window. Then I reach in, unlatch the screen, and push it out of the window. I'm in!

Right away I hear a thump in the hall, which really scares me because I checked and both cars were gone from the garage, meaning they're not home. Who could it be? I drop to the floor and watch from under my bed, and here comes Tiger trotting into the room with her big tail sticking in the air. She walks right under the bed and sniffs me. I give her my special chin rub, and she starts purring. Nobody rubs her like I do.

Now what? I figured that at least Jeff would be here since he doesn't work, and I could fix things with him. Then he'd talk to Laurie and they'd both talk to Al and her boss and everything would be fine. Now I don't know what to do. Nothing ever works out like I planned. I could just lie back in my bed and when they come home say, "Hi, what's up?" like I never left. Maybe they'd pretend too, and Al could pretend and the whole mess would go away. I wish adults would pretend more. It would make fixing situations a lot easier.

Whatever I do I have to remember to hold Tiger on my lap. They could never throw me out if I'm holding her.

"Andy?"

What? Where am I waking up now?

"Andy—what are you doing here?"

They're standing over me with strange expressions, like they thought I was dead and I just came alive. I can't tell from their faces if they're angry at seeing me or just surprised. It's time to try pretending. "Why shouldn't I be here? It's my room, isn't it?"

"How did you get here?" Laurie says. "Did Alison bring you?"

"No, I took the train, which was the first time by myself. I didn't have to ask anybody for help either." I figure that's pretty good for a twelve year old to do by himself. She should be proud of me, right?

"You took the train to Concord? Then how did you get here?"

"I walked. I counted my steps and I took two thousand and twenty-two. Do you think that's two miles?" They look at each other, then back at me. They don't know what to say. That's good. "What's for dinner anyway? I'm starving. Walking made me hungry."

"You ran away?" Laurie says.

"It's not really running away because this is my home and you can't run away *to* your home, right?"

"I don't think Alison's going to buy that logic," Laurie says.

Ted! I lean over the side of the bed and grab for his arm. He's covered in dust and cat hair, so I have to brush him off. "How come you left him under the bed?"

"We didn't know he was there," she says. "He didn't say anything."

It's not a very funny joke, but I laugh anyway. Jeff isn't laughing. He hasn't said a word to me. He's just staring out of the window. Why can't he look at me? Please, look at me! I'm sorry I caused all the trouble. I really am. If he'd look at me he'd see that.

"We have to tell Alison you're here," he says, "and call the Brighton Boys Home too. They'll be worried about you."

I pull the blanket over Ted and me. Why couldn't we just do over the day last week he tried to get me out of bed? I'd get up this time. A kid should have a second chance.

"You can't hide," Jeff says. "You know your social worker will look for you here."

Why is he taking Al's side? Why can't he understand that I'm sorry I was rotten and got him in trouble? I don't want to be rotten. I could learn to be better. But they can't expect me to change overnight. Jeff's a teacher—why doesn't he teach me!

I knew this would happen. I knew I'd get to like them and then something would go wrong and bang—they'd send me away. "I wish I never came here. Why didn't you just make your own freaking baby and leave me alone?"

They don't say anything for a minute. I can hear them breathing.

"I can't have children," Laurie finally says. "That's why we decided to adopt."

I throw the blanket off my head. This is just what I thought. "So you really wanted your own baby. Everyone wants a baby. Nobody wants to adopt a twelve year old. You just took me because you felt sorry for me."

"We did feel sorry for you," Jeff says, "but we wanted you too."

"Maybe you wanted me before, but not now just because I made up one stupid story about you."

"We do still want you," Laurie says, "but you have to want us too—and not just because you hate The Home."

"I do want you, okay? I told Al that."

"It's not enough to say the words. You have to treat us as your parents. You can't cry abuse every time we happen to brush into you or try to get you up. We're your mother

≥225≤

and father now. You have to accept that that means sometimes we're going to have to make you do things you don't want."

"Then keep me if you're my mother. Don't send me back 'cause I'll never get out of there. I know it."

They're both looking at the floor now. Why don't they say something?

"Please," I say to them, and Laurie looks up at me, then Jeff, "Please Mom and . . . *Dad*"—that's it, the magic word! "I'll call you that all the time, okay, Jeff? Except you're not like my old dad. He gave me up. You wouldn't do that. So I'll call you something else, like Pop."

They look at each other for a while, and I can tell they're talking to each other again without saying any words. I guess that happens when you've been married for a long time. "Okay, Andy," he says, "you've made a big effort to come back to us, and we'll do everything we can to keep you. That's a promise."

"Yes!" For once I've gotten something I asked for. All of a sudden I really am hungry. "So, what *is* for dinner?"

Things didn't get settled overnight. It took Jeff and Laurie couple of days to straighten out the mess with Alison and the DSS. We had meetings with the shrink and with the counselors at The Home and with Alison and her boss. Every time we went into an office, I sat between Jeff and Laurie so I could grab onto one of them if somebody tried to snatch me away. A couple of times I put my hand on his shoulder to show there's nothing wrong with touching like that.

They finally believed me that I lied about Jeff. That was strange—me trying to convince people I was *lying*. Usually I'm trying to make them believe I'm telling the truth.

One night after she read to me, Laurie said she hoped I had learned a lesson about how lies can hurt people. Just then Tiger came in my room and I scooped her into my arms. I thought about swearing on her life that I wouldn't lie ever again. But I'm not sure I can absolutely keep that promise, so I just crossed my heart and said I'd try as hard as I could to tell the truth, even if it got me in trouble.

EPILOGUE

IT'S THE FIRST day of spring, and today I'm getting my family for good.

I can't believe it—I've been living with Jeff and Laurie for more than six months. Today we go to court so they can officially adopt me. Laurie said I was adopting them too—as parents—and I guess that's true.

I still think of them sometimes as Laurie and Jeff, but I try extra hard to call them Mom and Pop when I'm talking to them. It's not easy calling people that after you've had other parents for so long. It feels a little like I'm being a traitor to my first mom and dad. But I figure that if they didn't want me as their kid anymore, I should be free to get other parents.

After Jeff and Laurie took me back from The Home, I acted better than perfect for a while. I was really scared that I'd mess up again and they'd be sorry for giving me another chance. So I did everything they said right away, and I finished all my homework without their nagging me, and I cleaned up the garage before they asked me. Al said I was going through the honeymoon period, like after a wedding, when you're afraid to say or do anything wrong.

Honeymoons always end, Al said, and I'm glad mine did, because I was getting so nervous trying to be good that my stomach started aching. What happened is that I was slinging my yo-yo in the living room one day and Laurie told me not to.

I was really close to doing a perfect around-the-universe, which is a trick I invented that's way better than around-the-world. So I kept trying it for a few minutes. Then Jeff told me to stop too. When he left the room I gave around-the-universe one last try. My yo-yo spun out behind me in an awesome arc, but then it snapped off the string and sailed into the mirror over the mantel. They both came running and yelling at me. I said it wasn't my fault, because a yo-yo shouldn't come off its string, right? We could probably sue the yo-yo manufacturer. They didn't like that idea. Jeff said I'd have to pay for the mirror out of my allowance. Laurie sent me to my room for the rest of the afternoon for not obeying them.

The best thing was that while they were yelling at me and later when I was grounded in my room, I didn't think once about how they might kick me out because of this. I could get in trouble like any other kid, and I'd still have a family.

I told Harry and Sam and Katie and all my friends at school that I'd be skipping today because I'm being adopted this afternoon. Harry said I was lucky. I thought he meant because I get a day off, but he said, "You're lucky you get to live with two parents." I thought about that and he's right. Most of the kids have parents who are divorced and never speak to each other. Harry has to go back and forth between two houses—he spends the school week at his mother's and the weekend at his father's. He keeps wishing his parents would get back together, but he knows that's not going to happen. Some of the other kids have stepfathers or no fathers at all. Me, I'm getting one mother and one father all to myself. I guess I am lucky.

I already took my shower, so I'm not supposed to get dirty. But it's warm out and I can't stand being inside all morning. Besides, I want to tell someone else my news—Mr. Lucinski.

I haven't seen him at all over the winter, because he stays inside with that old dog of his. When I swing into his driveway on my bike, I spot him in his backyard, just like I expected. I'm kicking up stones under my tires and making a racket, but he doesn't hear me until I hop off my bike right next to him.

"Hey, Mr. L., what's up?"

He's sitting in his folding chair hunched over an old cradle that's half painted. He looks at the sky and shakes his head. "I don't see anything up." I don't think he's joking with me, but you can never be sure with Mr. Lucinski. Then he looks at me with those squinty eyes of his, like the way Superman looks through walls. "I haven't seen you for a while, boy," he says. "What are you running away from today?"

"That's what I came to tell you. I don't have to run anymore after today. I'm going to be theirs."

"Whose?"

"Theirs—you know, my new parents. I've been living with them for long enough and they're going to keep me. It'll be legal after we go to court and tell a judge we want to be a family."

He looks at me like I'm not making sense. I figure I should leave, but then he hands me a paintbrush. "I'd be selfish to keep all the pleasure to myself," he says. "Get that other chair to sit in and try your hand at it."

He's pointing underneath the porch where there's a beat-up old lawn chair that's been lying out all winter. He must be crazy—I'd have to crawl through mud and spiders and who knows what else to get it. Even if I wasn't all clean I wouldn't go under there. "I think I'll just kneel, Mr. L."

"Suit yourself," he says. "Just mind the dripping."

I don't know what that means, but it doesn't matter because I'm awesome at painting. Jeff taught me not to get the brush too wet and how to keep my painting hand steady by holding my wrist. I painted my whole room by myself.

So I dip into the white paint to do the base of the cradle and then switch to red for the roses and then to pink to start on the little floating babies on the side. It's easy coloring over what was already there.

"Where did you get this anyway?"

"It was my own cradle more than seventy years ago."

It's funny thinking of old man Lucinski curled up in this little wooden box, and his mother sticking a bottle in his mouth. I bet he spit up on her a lot. He probably huffed even back then.

"What're you laughing at, boy?"

"Nothing. How come you're painting this now?"

He lays down his brush and sits back in his chair like he's finished. "My granddaughter's just had her first, a little boy, so I thought she might like to have it."

"Oh." So I'm painting and he's looking over my shoulder, which is okay because he's not telling me to watch this and watch that—he's just looking and nodding and grunting. I figure he's pulling a Tom Sawyer on me, getting me to do his work, but I don't care because painting isn't work to me.

"That's good," he says as I finish doing the ugliest floating baby with its big round frog eyes. "It takes patience to paint."

"Are you sure it does, Mr. Lucinski? Because nobody ever said I had patience before. I got ADD, you know."

"*You* got AIDs?"

"No, ADD—it's Attention Deficit Disorder."

The old man looks at the cradle and at me. "And the doctors say you have it?"

"Yep."

"Well maybe they're just expecting you to have patience with the wrong things. That may be it."

"Yeah, maybe." I dip into the pink paint again to start the second floating ugly baby. After that I just have the clouds to do and then the cradle will be done. Mr. Lucinski pulls a cigar from his shirt pocket and sticks it in his mouth.

"You know you shouldn't be smoking, Mr. L. It's bad for you."

"What's it going to do? Stunt my growth?"

He laughs at his joke, and I laugh a little too.

"It can kill you."

"Well, dying's not the worst thing that could happen to me. I'm ready to go whenever it comes."

"But I don't want you to die yet. I haven't known you for long enough."

He takes the cigar from his mouth and stares at me. "You know, boy, that's the nicest thing anybody's said to me in a long time."

"Can I ask you something, Mr. L.?"

"Can't stop you."

"How come people think you're mean?"

He looks at me surprised, and I think maybe I shouldn't have asked him that. "I didn't know they did," he says.

"Oh yeah, my pop thinks you're wicked cold."

"Wicked cold?"

"It means not very friendly. I made it up."

He huffs at me. "There's nothing you can say that hasn't been said before."

That doesn't sound true. I know I can think of something. "How about, If the sky weren't up it would be down and the ground would be up and the stars would come out in the ground and the grass would grow in the sky? I bet nobody in the history of anywhere ever said that before."

The old man stares at me. His lips start opening, and I think he's going to laugh, which I never saw him do before. But then he coughs a few times and throws his cigar down on the ground. "Why, boy, it's amazing," he says, "but I was saying that exact thing to myself just the other day."

I don't believe it. So I'm staring him down and after a

minute he can't help laughing. Then I start laughing so hard that I knock over the can of pink paint onto his boots, and we just laugh some more.

They make me dress up for court. Mom gives the orders—the blue button-down shirt she just bought for me; pants, not jeans, with no ragged cuffs from skateboarding; shoes, too, not sneakers; my old school blazer. And no chain in my pocket!

She lays out the clothes on my bed and tells me to hurry so she can see how everything fits.

When I pull on the clothes and stand in front of the mirror, I can't believe it. I look like a preppy. José would die laughing if he saw me like this.

"Can I come in, Andy?"

I open the door for Pop, and I can tell from his face that I look terrible. He opens the top button of my shirt so I can breathe better and tugs at my pants to make them a little baggier. "I'd lose the jacket," he says. "It's about three years too small for you."

I slip out of the jacket and toss it on the bed. Then I take another peek in the mirror. "I still look like a dork."

He laughs at that and throws his arm around my shoulder. "But soon you'll be *our* dork."

It's my day in court.

Dad told me that if I ever go in front of a judge, I should look sad and say, "Yes, sir," to everything. No matter what the judge says, I'm supposed to say, "Yes, sir."

Al reaches over and stops me from bouncing Ted on the bench. "There's no reason to be nervous," she says. "This will only take a few minutes."

Me nervous? I'm just changing my whole life, that's all.

A guy in a uniform sticks his head out of the room and says the judge is ready for us. He holds the door open, and they all wait for me to go in. But I'm not going in there first, so Al does, then Mom and Pop and me.

What a room! There are huge windows on the side and giant pictures of old men in black robes hanging on the walls. Everything smells old. We go through a little gate and sit behind a table, just the four of us, plus Ted. Sitting high up in front of us is the judge, but it's not a he, it's a she.

"Hey, Al, where is everybody?"

She leans across to whisper to me. "This is a private hearing, Andy, no one else is allowed in."

So I'm sitting in between my almost-parents, and all of a sudden I feel like I got gas that's going to bust out of me any second. God, who would want a kid that stinks up the courtroom?

"Good morning," the judge says. We all say good morning back at her. She starts on some long speech about why we're here, and Al hands over papers for her to look at. Then the judge says, "Andrew, I understand you've been living with the Sizeracys for six months. Is that right?"

"Yes, sir . . . I mean . . ."—quick Fleck, what do you call a woman judge? "I mean, just yes."

"Don't be nervous," she says.

Why does everybody tell me that?

"I see that you live in Concord," she says. "What's your home like?"

"It's like a home with different rooms in it."

"Do you have your own bedroom?"

"Oh yeah, and it's pretty cool 'cause I have my posters all over. And there's a big yard out back with lots of trees. And there's my cat, Tiger. She catches everything and kills it and we have a pail of all the killed stuff, which is pretty gross."

"I see," the judge says. "How are you doing in school?"

I look at Pop and he looks at me because I'm not doing too hot. I'm getting Ds in science and history because I keep forgetting to hand my homework in. "I have perfect attendance—except for today."

"That's good to hear. How about your grades?"

"I'm not F-ing anything—I mean flunking. But I could do better. I'm figuring on doing better pretty soon."

The judge smiles, which surprises me because I didn't think they were allowed to do that.

"Mr. and Mrs. Sizeracy, you understand that adopting Andrew means that under statute he will be your legal son, and you bear all the responsibilities toward him of any child born naturally to you?"

"We understand," they say.

"Andrew," the judge says, "you're thirteen years old now, and that means that you get to say yes or no to this adoption. I won't agree to it unless it's something you want."

Of course I want it. Why else would I be standing here dressed like a dork? "Oh yeah, I want it."

"All right," she says. "The papers are in order, so I will now execute the adoption of Andrew Thomas Fleck by Laraine and Jeffrey Sizeracy of Concord, Massachusetts, and concurrently, the change of name to Andrew Thomas Sizeracy."

After she signs the papers she hands them to Al and she signs and then Mom and Pop do. "Don't I get to sign anything?"

The judge pushes her glasses down her nose. "I suppose it does seem odd," she says. "You're the only one who doesn't have to sign a paper."

"Yeah, it's pretty dumb."

"Who's that you have with you?"

"Oh, this is Ted."

"That bear must be very important to you," the judge says.

Of course Ted's important. He's gone with me through all my homes. Ted's seen everything I've seen and I don't care if it is dopey for a kid my age to have a stuffed animal, I'm keeping him forever. "Yeah, Ted's important."

The judge smiles again. "Well then, congratulations and good luck to all of you, including Ted."

Everybody stands up and starts shaking hands, so I guess it's over. Good-bye, Fleck, nice knowing you. Now you're Andy Sizeracy. Wait till I see José and he says, "Hey, Fleck." I'll bust him on that.

Alison gives me a big hug and says she's going to miss seeing me. What does she think, I'm going to the moon? "You can see me anytime you want, Al. Just come visit."

Then Mom throws her arms around me and hugs so hard I think I'm going to throw up breakfast. After her, Pop shakes my hand and punches me in the shoulder. I think that's all he's going to do, but then he grabs me in a bear hug and says, "I wish we could have been your parents from the beginning." He squeezes extra hard when he says this, and for the first time in my life, I'm not afraid to squeeze back.

I knew somebody would want me. I wasn't worried for a minute.

GEORGE HARRAR is the author of *First Tiger,* a novel about a teenage runaway returning home. His short fiction has appeared in numerous magazines for children and adults. His short story "The 5:22" won *Story* magazine's Carson McCullers Prize and was selected for the 1999 edition of *The Best American Short Stories.*

Harrar grew up in Jenkintown, Pennsylvania, and now lives in Wayland, Massachusetts, with his wife, Linda, a documentary filmmaker. They have one son, Tony.

IF YOU ENJOYED THIS BOOK, YOU'LL ALSO WANT TO
READ THESE OTHER MILKWEED NOVELS.

To order books or for more information, contact Milkweed at
(800) 520-6455 or visit our website (www.milkweed.org).

THE $66 SUMMER
by John Armistead

MILKWEED PRIZE FOR CHILDREN'S LITERATURE
NEW YORK PUBLIC LIBRARY BEST BOOKS OF THE YEAR:
    "BOOKS FOR THE TEEN AGE"

In the summer of 1955, when George Harrington's grandmother invites him to visit and help out at her store in small-
town Obadiah, Alabama, he sees a way to earn money for the
Harley-Davidson motorcycle he wants. When he gets there,
George befriends Esther and Bennett, the children of the cook
at his grandmother's lunch counter. While fishing and adven-
turing together on the neighbor's land, they uncover chilling
evidence of a forgotten crime. As currents of racism and
bigotry come to the town's surface, George must reassess his
priorities and learn what sacrifice is all about.

GILDAEN, THE HEROIC ADVENTURES OF A MOST
UNUSUAL RABBIT
by Emilie Buchwald

CHICAGO TRIBUNE BOOK FESTIVAL AWARD, BEST BOOK FOR AGES 9–12

Gildaen is befriended by a mysterious being who has lost his
memory but not the ability to change shape at will. Together
they accept the perilous task of thwarting the evil sorcerer,
Grimald, in this tale of magic, villainy, and heroism.

THE OCEAN WITHIN
by V. M. Caldwell

MILKWEED PRIZE FOR CHILDREN'S LITERATURE

Elizabeth is a foster child who has just been placed with the boisterous and affectionate Sheridans, a family that wants to adopt her. Used to having to look out for herself, however, Elizabeth is reluctant to open up to them. During a summer spent by the ocean with the eight Sheridan children and their grandmother, who Elizabeth dubs "Iron Woman" because of her strict discipline, Elizabeth learns what it means—and how much she must risk—to become a permanent member of a loving family.

TIDES
by V. M. Caldwell

Recently adopted twelve-year-old Elizabeth Sheridan is looking forward to spending the summer at Grandma's oceanside home. But on her stay there, she faces problems involving her cousins, five-year-old Petey and eighteen-year-old Adam, that cause her to question whether the family will hold together. As she and Grandma help each other through troubling times, Elizabeth comes to see that she has become an important member of the family.

NO PLACE
by Kay Haugaard

Arturo Morales and his fellow sixth-grade classmates decide to improve their neighborhood and their lives by building a park in their otherwise concrete, inner-city Los Angeles barrio. The kids are challenged by their teachers to figure out what it would take to transform the neighborhood junkyard into a clean, safe place for children to play. Despite their parents' skepticism and the threat of street gangs, Arturo and his classmates struggle to prove that the actions of individuals—even kids—can make a difference.

BUSINESS AS USUAL
by David Haynes
from the West 7th Wildcats Series

In Mr. Harrison's sixth-grade class, the West 7th Wildcats must learn how to run a business. Kevin Olsen, one of the Wildcats as well as the class clown, is forced out of the Wildcat group and into an unwilling alliance working in a group with the Wildcats' nemesis, Jenny Pederson. In the process of making staggering amounts of cookies for Marketplace Day, the classmates venture into the realm of free enterprise, discovering more than they imagined about business, the world, and themselves.

THE GUMMA WARS
by David Haynes
from the West 7th Wildcats Series

MAUDE HART LOVELACE AWARD FINALIST

Larry "Lu" Underwood and his fellow West 7th Wildcats have been looking forward to Tony Rodriguez's birthday fiesta all year—only to discover that Lu must also spend the day with his two feuding "gummas," the name he gave his grandmothers when he was just learning to talk. The two "gummas," Gumma Jackson and Gumma Underwood, are hostile to one another, especially when it comes to claiming the affection of their only grandson. On the action-packed day of Tony's birthday, Lu, a friend, and the gummas find themselves exploring the sights of Minneapolis and St. Paul—and eventually find themselves enjoying each other's company.

THE MONKEY THIEF
by Aileen Kilgore Henderson

NEW YORK PUBLIC LIBRARY BEST BOOKS OF THE YEAR:
"BOOKS FOR THE TEEN AGE"

Twelve-year-old Steve Hanson is sent to Costa Rica for eight months to live with his uncle. There he discovers a world completely unlike anything he can see from the cushions of his couch back home, a world filled with giant trees and insects, mysterious sounds, and the constant companionship of monkeys swinging in the branches overhead. When Steve hatches a plan to capture a monkey for himself, his quest for a pet leads him into dangerous territory. It takes all of Steve's survival skills—and the help of his new friends—to get him out of trouble.

THE SUMMER OF THE BONEPILE MONSTER
by Aileen Kilgore Henderson

MILKWEED PRIZE FOR CHILDREN'S LITERATURE
ALABAMA LIBRARY ASSOCIATION 1996 JUVENILE/YOUNG ADULT AWARD
MAUDE HART LOVELACE AWARD FINALIST

Eleven-year-old Hollis Orr has been sent to spend the summer with Grancy, his father's grandmother, in rural Dolliver, Alabama, while his parents "work things out." As summer begins, Hollis encounters a road called Bonepile Hollow, barred by a gate and a real skull and bones mounted on a board. "Things that go down that road don't ever come back," he is told. Thus begins the mystery that plunges Hollis into real danger.

TREASURE OF PANTHER PEAK
by Aileen Kilgore Henderson

NEW YORK PUBLIC LIBRARY BEST BOOKS OF THE YEAR: "BOOKS FOR THE TEEN AGE"

Twelve-year-old Page Williams begrudgingly accompanies her mother, Ellie, as she flees her abusive husband, Page's father. Together they settle in a fantastic new world—Big Bend National Park, Texas. Wild animals stalk through the park, and the nearby Ghost Mountains are filled with legends of lost treasures. As Page tests her limits by sneaking into forbidden canyons, Ellie struggles to win the trust of other parents. Only through their newfound courage are they able to discover a treasure beyond what they could have imagined.

I AM LAVINA CUMMING
by Susan Lowell

MOUNTAINS & PLAINS BOOKSELLERS ASSOCIATION AWARD

In 1905, ten-year-old Lavina is sent from her home on the Bosque Ranch in Arizona Territory to live with her aunt in the city of Santa Cruz, California. Armed with the Cumming family motto, "courage," Lavina deals with a new school, homesickness, a very spoiled cousin, an earthquake, and a big decision about her future.

THE BOY WITH PAPER WINGS
by Susan Lowell

Confined to bed with a viral fever, eleven-year-old Paul sails a paper airplane into his closet and propels himself into mysterious and dangerous realms in this exciting and fantastical adventure. Paul finds himself trapped in the military diorama on his closet floor, out to stop the evil commander, KRON. Armed only with paper and the knowledge of how to fold it, Paul uses his imagination and courage to find his way out of dilemmas and disasters.

THE SECRET OF THE RUBY RING
by Yvonne MacGrory

IRISH CHILDREN'S BOOK TRUST
BISTO "BOOK OF THE YEAR" AWARD

Lucy gets a very special birthday present, a star ruby ring, from her grandmother and finds herself transported to Langley Castle in the Ireland of 1885. At first, she is intrigued by castle life, in which she is the lowliest servant, until she loses the ruby ring and her only way home.

A BRIDE FOR ANNA'S PAPA
by Isabel R. Marvin

MILKWEED PRIZE FOR CHILDREN'S LITERATURE

Life on Minnesota's Iron Range in 1907 is not easy for thirteen-year-old Anna Kallio. Her mother's death has left Anna to take care of the house, her young brother, and her father, a blacksmith in the dangerous iron mines. So she and her brother plot to find their father a new wife, even attempting to arrange a match with one of the "mail order" brides arriving from Finland.

MINNIE
by Annie M. G. Schmidt

THE NETHERLANDS' SILVER PENCIL PRIZE:
  ONE OF THE BEST BOOKS OF THE YEAR

Miss Minnie is a cat. Or rather, she *was* a cat. She is now a
human, and she's not at all happy to be one. As Minnie tries
to find and reverse the cause of her transformation, she
brings her reporter friend, Mr. Tibbs, news from the cats'
gossip hotline—including revealing information that one
of the town's most prominent citizens is not the animal lover
he appears to be.

THE DOG WITH GOLDEN EYES
by Frances Wilbur

MILKWEED PRIZE FOR CHILDREN'S LITERATURE
TEXAS LONE STAR READING LIST

Many girls dream of owning a dog of their own, but Cassie's
wish for one takes an unexpected turn in this contemporary
tale of friendship and growing up. Thirteen-year-old Cassie is
lonely, bored, and feeling friendless when a large, beautiful
dog appears one day in her suburban backyard. Cassie wants
to adopt the dog, but as she learns more about him, she realizes that she is, in fact, caring for a full-grown Arctic wolf. As
she attempts to protect the wolf from urban dangers, Cassie
discovers that she possesses strengths and resources she
never imagined.

BEHIND THE BEDROOM WALL
by Laura E. Williams

It is 1942. Thirteen-year-old Korinna Rehme is an active member of her local *Jungmädel,* a Nazi youth group, along with many of her friends. Korinna's parents, however, secretly are members of an underground group providing a means of escape to the Jews of their city and are, in fact, hiding a refugee family behind the wall of Korinna's bedroom. As Korinna comes to know the family, and their young daughter, her sympathies begin to turn. But when someone tips off the Gestapo, loyalties are put to the test and Korinna must decide in what she believes and whom she trusts.

THE SPIDER'S WEB
by Laura E. Williams

Thirteen-year-old Lexi Jordan has just joined The Pack, a group of neo-Nazi skinheads, as a substitute for the family she wishes she had. After she and The Pack spray paint a synagogue, Lexi hides from her pursuers on the front porch of elderly Ursula Zeidler, a former member of the Hitler Youth Group, who painfully recalls her ugly anti-Semitic Nazi activities and betrayal of a friend that she bitterly rues.

When her younger sister becomes enthralled with Lexi's new "family," Lexi realizes the true meaning of The Pack and has little time to save herself and her sister from its sinister grip.

MILKWEED EDITIONS publishes with the intention of making a humane impact on society, in the belief that literature is a transformative art uniquely able to convey the essential experiences of the human heart and spirit. To that end, Milkweed publishes distinctive voices of literary merit in handsomely designed, visually dynamic books, exploring the ethical, cultural, and esthetic issues that free societies need continually to address. Milkweed Editions is a not-for-profit press.

JOIN US

Milkweed publishes adult and children's fiction, poetry and, in its World As Home program, literary nonfiction about the natural world. Milkweed also hosts two websites: www.milkweed.org, where readers can find in-depth information about Milkweed books, authors, and programs, and www.worldashome.org, which is your online resource of books, organizations, and writings that explore ethical, esthetic, and cultural dimensions of our relationship to the natural world.

Since its genesis as *Milkweed Chronicle* in 1979, Milkweed has helped hundreds of emerging writers reach their readers. Thanks to the generosity of foundations and of individuals like you, Milkweed Editions is able to continue its nonprofit mission of publishing books chosen on the basis of literary merit—of how they impact the human heart and spirit—rather than on how they impact the bottom line. That's a miracle that our readers have made possible.

In addition to purchasing Milkweed books, you can join the growing community of Milkweed supporters. Individual contributions of any amount are both meaningful and welcome. Contact us for a Milkweed catalog or log on to www.milkweed.org and click on "About Milkweed," then "Why Join Milkweed," to find out about our donor program, or simply call (800) 520-6455 and ask about becoming one of Milkweed's contributors. As a non-profit press, Milkweed belongs to you, the community. Milkweed's board, its staff, and especially the authors whose careers you help launch thank you for reading our books and supporting our mission in any way you can.

Interior design by Dale Cooney
Typeset in Scala 10.5/15
by Stanton Publication Services
Printed on acid-free 50# Frasier Trade Natural paper
by Friesen Corporation